UNTOLD STORY: FROM LOLLIPOP KID TO MUNCHKIN KING

First edition. May 1, 2024.

Copyright © 2024 Michael T Ernst.

ISBN: 978-1736401514

Written by Michael T Ernst.

I0549947

Table of Contents

Dedicated to Jerry Maren, a very good friend. May he rest in peace.

Munchkins Lollipop Club, LLC
667 Holly Hill Drive
Casselberry, Florida 32707

Publishers note: This is a work of fiction. Names, characters, places, and incidents are a product of the author's imagination. Locales and public names are sometimes used for atmospheric purposes. Any resemblance to actual people, living or dead, or to businesses, companies, events, institutions, or locales is completely coincidental.

Book design © 2020 BookdesignTemplates.com

Ordering information: Special discounts are available on quantity purchases by corporations, associations, and others. For details, contact the Publisher listed at the address above.

ISBN # 978-1-736-40151-4

FORWARD

The year was 1938, The place was Boston, MA. I was.
seventeen years old and just three feet, seven inches tall. I was a little person. There was no such word as "munchkin' back in those days! A man in a three-piece suit approached me behind the curtains after my state performance. He told me that he represented Lowe's.
Incorporated and asked me if I wanted to be "The Lollipop Kid" Munchkin and participate in their upcoming new move, "The Wizard of OZ!" I said to myself, "What is a munchkin?" and "What is a Lollipop Kid?" I did not get to ask him because I did not want him to know how stupid I really was! As you can guess, I quickly said.
"Yes!" and off I was on the next bus to Hollywood!
Filming "The Wizard of Oz" was the first of many movies that I made during the next seven decades. I remained on the West Coast and filmed a few "Our Gang" comedies and was quickly featured in a role starring the Marx Brothers, called "At the Circus." The rest of my life is history. Anyway, I have been contacted hundreds of times by the acting community with offers of work, be it some sort of film or television commercial. I always wondered when I would receive a phone call or letter in the mail asking me to act in a sequel to the "Wizard of Oz." This has NEVER happened, and I understand why.
Basically, how could you successfully produce a sequel for the number one movie of the century, a movie that has been viewed by SEVEN out of TEN adults? Did you know that "The Wizard of Oz" movie has been viewed by FIVE out of a HUNDRED adults more than TEN times? Also, it was filmed in over THIRTY different languages. Also, that the movie has been seen by over THREE BILLION people around the world! Let me simply answer my own question. YOU DON'T! It is impossible to film a sequel to "The Wizard of Oz!" There has never been any movie filmed, nor will there ever by a film produced in the future that will capture the minds and the hearts of both young and old alike, as did "The Wizard of Oz" .... except...until.... NOW!
I am confident that "The Untold Story: From Lollipop Kid to Munchkin King" might just be the one book that could be made into a movie sequel to "The Wizard of Oz." This newest story, written by my dear friend Michael T. Ernst with a little help from me, allows the reader's imagination to journey the adventurous of paths of five Munchkin teenagers and their Munchkin Granny. These Munchkins are "not off to see the Wizard," but off to find the Warlock in an attempt to locate, destroy and recover his magical medallion. Finding it will reverse the Warlock's evil curse that he placed on the town of Munchkin land to avenge the deaths of his two sisters, the Wicked Witches of the East, and the West seventy-five years earlier!
t was under this disguise of a relaxing dinner that "The Untold Story: From Lollipop Kid to Munchkin King" was first told to me by Michael, an extremely talented inventor and storyteller. Michael explained to me his adventure story. Right from the beginning, I was impressed with his style, possessing both a touch of personal humor with a twist of unique excitement, which made me just crave to pick his brain for more.

The rest is history. Michael told me his tale. I believe that someday in the near future (I hope it is soon, I just turned 86 years old, and I am not getting' any younger!), that I will receive my long-awaited phone call or letter in the mail asking me to act in Michael's book-turned into-movie, "The Untold Story: From Lollipop Kid to Munchkin King".

So, come out, come out, wherever you are! Tighten your seatbelts and join me and the rest of my Munchkin friends as we "go down in history" and begin our exciting journey with "The Untold Story: From Lollipop Kid to Munchkin King."

Jerry Maren, The Lollipop Kid Munchkin extraordinaire!

MUNCHKIN PROMISE

My promise to Jerry Maren, The Lollipop Kid, was made during the toy fair in New York City in the early 2000's. I was walking around he exhibits when I felt a tug on the back of my coat. I turned around to see a small lady looking up at me. She said, "You like to meet the Lollipop Kid from the Wizard of Oz Movie?"

I replied, "I would love too!" So, she introduced herself as Elizabeth, the wife of the Lollipop Kid, she took my hand and lead me to a table where her husband Jerry was sitting.

During my visit with Jerry, we talked about many things, but the one question I asked him was, "Why was there never a movie about the Munchkins?" Jerry smiled and replied, "Because no one ever has come up with a story." This puzzled me, so I said to Jerry, "I am a toy inventor and I feel I could make a board game about the Munchkins and if I did, would he support the idea." Jerry said, "Yes, I would love to see a game about the Munchkins!"

So, I promised him in one year I would return and show him the boardgame. We shook hands and agreed to meet again.

One year later I returned to the toy fair to find Jerry. I showed him my printout of the Munchkin board game, but during the making of the game, I had decided to make up a story. I told him my idea, he smiled at me and said, "I love the idea and I will help you in the adventure." We met a few times after that, but it took me longer to make a board game and to also write that book and during that time my friend Jerry died before he could see this book. I have kept my promise to him, and this book is dedicated to Jerry Maren and his wife Elizabeth. May he Rest in Peace!

Restfully, Michael T. Ernst.

UNTOLD STORY:

FROM LOLLIPOP KID
TO
MUNCHKING KING

CHAPTER 1

FREEDOM CELEBRATION

A famous city that is the heart of stories told around the world with blinding emerald filled skies above a city so breathtaking it can only be described as truly majestic. Despite how wonderful this place may be though, this is a tale of a town dwarfed in the shadows of its glorified neighboring city, Oz. Located on this small piece of land, just a little over two hundred cheerful people known as the Munchkins gather in the town square to start their annual Freedom celebration. In the center of town stands a grand wooden platform strategically placed so that everyone in the magical village can hear and see what is unfolding. Once everyone was seated on the soft grass, a horn sounded from the King's house, which happened to overlook the only road in town. The King appeared wearing a long, red velvet cloak and smooth black boots and the most magnificent crown adorned his head. Its gems and jewels were so beautiful and rare and gave every eye cause to stop and stare. As the King approached the platform, his cloak swaying and his crown glistening in the afternoon sun, the crowd came alive with cheers. He paused momentarily to scan his small sea of citizens then settled on his throne.

"Thank you, my fellow Munchkins!" The King began.

"Your cheers fill the air on this beautiful day bringing me so much joy, there are no words." Quietly the crowd began to turn their full attention to the words being spoken from the platform.

"This glorious day marks 75 years of freedom from the Evil Witch who tormented us from the West", declared the King.

"Ding-Dong the Witch is dead" rang out from the band and everyone began to sing. After some time, a small, yet brilliant light appeared and as it drew nearer, the shimmering light directed itself towards the King. The King smiled as the ball landed beside him and morphed into Glinda, The Good Witch of the North. The King knew Glinda and her sister, the Good Witch of the South since he was a young boy and he greeted her with a hug; The King welcomed the Good Witch to their humble town.

"It is so good to see you again, as you are my favorite King in all the lands," Glinda smiled.

"Must I keep asking you to PLEASE not call me 'King'?" asked the King adding "Just call me Jerry, okay?"

"Okay Jerry, you call me Glinda and we have a deal!"

Glinda playfully stated. They both laughed and agreed. Two stagehands suddenly appeared with a chair for the Good Witch to sit upon.

"Well, Happy Birthday to you Jerry," Glinda shouted. She raised her magic wand; everyone watched with amazement because any magic the wand performed was wonderful to look at, out of it burst a light that shot to the skies filling it with brilliant fireworks.

As all eyes watched in delight at the blue, green, and silver glitter raining down from the sky nobody noticed the small group of teenage Munchkins carrying rods and sneaking off to do a little moonlight fishing. Within this group there was an inventor, though only seventeen, who chose to take an optimistic approach to life and known to all his friends as Mikey. Mikey considered himself an expert at envisioning things in a unique and creative way. Following close behind in age was the very pretty, young Munchkin named Zee, a 16-year-old, sharply dressed cheerleader that was not afraid of taking chances. Next was Maven, a mature 14-year-old, who loves hunting and could knock the hole of a Munchkin donut with his bow and arrow. Then there is Puff, who was close to turning 13 years old, slightly overweight and a lover of all things sweet, but most of all he adored his home-made Munchkin bars and would do anything for cookies or candy. Puff had a special talent; just before any danger approached, he would start sneezing uncontrollably. Finally, there was Maria, 11 years old, the owner of a magical Siamese cat she called SarCat. Maria named him SarCat because of his unusual sarcastic speaking manner. SarCat was eternally devoted to Maria, loyalty as well as a protective nature which kept him close behind Maria thwarting off any harm that came her way.

UNTOLD STORY: FROM LOLLIPOP KID TO MUNCHKIN KING

After successfully making it to the front gate unnoticed by anyone in the crowd, Maven stated, "We are in luck! No gate keeper!"

Out of nowhere, a familiar yet stern voice stated, "Where do you think you are going?" Scared to bits, the teenagers all began to look around desperately for the voice that spoke to them.

"Granny!" exclaimed Zee, "You scared us!!"

"I am the gatekeeper this evening and I would like to know what you kids are up to?" Granny asked.

"We are not kids anymore" Zee defended. "The moon is full and exactly right so we thought we could do a little moonlight fishing. Completely harmless," Zee informed her. Zee further reasoned, "Besides, who wants to sit around listening to the King tell tales of Evil Witches that never existed!"

"You, my dear, have a lot to learn," Granny scolded. She reached over and took the fishing pole out of Mikey's hand, a faraway look crossed through her eyes as she was taken to a different place and time. She then hinted slightly to the kids, "Boy, it has been ages since I went full-moon fishing."

An unspoken agreement was made amongst the group with an exchange of glances.

Zee spoke for all, "Would you like to join us, Granny?"

"Why yes, I surely would! Just give me a minute to get my walking cane from the gate watcher room." Granny turned away to fetch her cane, moments later returning to the group.

"I sure hope nobody notices that the gate is unguarded." Granny stated. Reaching into her pocket to reveal a large rustic key that she put inside the lock and with some effort turned it until a faint click let them know that the gate was unlocked, and they all walked out, confirming she secured the gate. Granny stayed close to her cherished granddaughter, Zee, thinking to herself, "Now I know I can keep a watchful eye on her."

SarCat spoke in a high voice, "I think we should stay here!"

"Oh, you are a scaredy cat," said Maria to him as she bent down and patted her shoulder, signaling to SarCat that he was welcome to jump up there for a ride. SarCat happily obliged and landed gracefully on Maria's narrow shoulders.

"Now SarCat, be quiet! If we walk quickly, we are just a few hours away from the fishing hole," she told her beloved cat. The King's voice faded into the distance along with the town as the group set out on their journey.

Deep in an underground cave sat a castle ten stories high, built from the hottest stones to be found. There lived a nameless Warlock so corrupt and dastardly no single word could begin to describe his evilness. He was a tall man dressed in black with a long blood-red velvet cape and was the brother of both the Wicked Witch of the West and the Wicked Witch of the East. Dangling from his neck was a powerful sort of magic in the form of a medallion, not the same magic that sends fireworks into the sky in celebration but an evil magic bringing no form of good to anyone. Choosing a place where only the most horrific evil would live, his castle burned as red as his passion for the tyranny he plotted against the town of Munchkins. Rooms filled his home waiting to be used by those with only the evilest of hearts. He sat there alone, thinking and planning because he knew it was time to make his move.

Monstrously tall creatures peaking at 9 feet tall form an army outside the grand wooden doors of Warlock's domain. The doors swing open before Warlock; he steps out taking a moment to drink in the sights of so many beings waiting to do any command he sends their way. Slowly, he walks out to face his soldiers, ugly as they were with their dragon heads and gorilla bodies, with long lizard tails swaying with each step they take and boney wings that have matted feathers adorning their backs ready to take them into flight at any moment. Standing upright in a human-like stance, they listened obediently as their master spoke.

"Seventy-five years ago, today, I suffered the loss of both of my sisters at the hands of Dorothy, the visitor from a faraway land and those despicable Munchkins," Warlock boomed, his words dripping with disgust and hatred. "Dorothy may have escaped the fate I had in store for her, but those Munchkins will not be so lucky!"
Cheers erupted from the army.
"The one they call Jerry still lives! We will fly to the land of Munchkins and avenge my sisters!"
Their hands were on fancy belts that were equipped with net shooting rifles, the dragon soldiers began to jump up and down with excitement.
Placing one hand around his medallion, the Warlock spoke in a loud clear voice, "Take me to the town of Munchkin!"
Then a sudden burst of wind whisked through the sea of soldiers and a tornado formed, engulfing Warlock, and transporting him from his underground

dwelling into the open towards his desired destination. Not far behind him, his dominions took flight blanketing the sky in one massive movement.

"Are we nearly there yet or are we going to have to wait for the sun to set and rise again first?" SarCat inquired in his typical saucy manner.

They were making excellent time and Mikey reassured him of that, "Relax, my impatient feline friend, we are almost there."

"Boy am I hungry! How about a snack?" Puff asked.

"That does not sound like a bad idea," Mikey agreed.

Everyone prepared his own snacks to take along on the trip and since Granny was added later, Zee was more than willing to share hers. Sitting down next to Granny, she gave her half of what she had. While resting their tired feet and now with satisfied bellies Puff out of nowhere broke into a sneezing fit. Everyone began looking around for the imminent danger that their friends sneezing attack invariably indicated was heading their way.

"Look! A tornado!" yelled Zee, "And it's coming this way!"

"Everyone take cover and keep your voices low," whispered Granny. "That tornado has ears." The kids all looked at Granny with puzzled expressions.

"What kind of tornado is that?" questioned Maven in a low tone.

"I'm not sure what kind it is but it looks as though there is something in it," replied Mikey.

It was getting harder and harder to see as dust clouded the air around them and winds whipped in every direction. After several minutes of waiting, the Munchkin kids were left unharmed by the passing tornado. The town of Munchkins, however, was in the direct path of the flying menace and all the things whirling around behind it as it made its way straight for town. Music echoed throughout the town of Munchkin as the people danced together in the grass. Freedom Day was something that they all cherished, and it showed in their glee. A great joy filled Jerry and Glinda's ears as they sat upon the platform watching the festivities. As with all good things, they must come to an end. Suddenly, the Good Witch had a very bad feeling. She could sense danger on its way, and she shot up out of her chair.

"Silence the music!" Shouted Glinda

Baffled, Jerry stood up beside her and exclaimed, "What is wrong? What is it?"

"Prepare your army for battle my friend. Evil is on its way to town, and we must be ready." Glinda said to Jerry.

Taking her words of caution very seriously, Jerry commanded to his army, "Great Munchkin army, take your posts along the surrounding walls and protect our great town! Everyone else takes shelter in your homes and await the return of our brave soldiers."

Powerful alarms filled the air as the soldiers took their stand along the wall and waited for an unknown evil determined to bring danger into their land.

The King's loyal general, a short, stocky Munchkin with a leadership ability to match his looks, soon saw the danger they sensed. "A tornado! Prepare your weapons!" Dutifully the army readied themselves and took aim waiting for the command to fire. When it reached barely fifty feet from the town walls, the general gave his order, "FIRE!!" in a booming voice far too big for his Munchkin size. To their dismay the bullets had no effect on the tornado and the order was given to cease fire. Never seeing their weapons perform so uselessly, they just stood there and waited, prepared to do whatever they must to protect their loved ones within the walls. A puff of smoke arose when the small tornado finally stopped spinning. Out of it appeared an all-slender man dressed in all black except for the creepy red cape draped over his shoulders.

CHAPTER 2

WHAT'S HAPPENING?

"I think that tornado hit our town," cried Maria.

"Did you see those flying things behind the tornado? What could those have been?" asked Puff.

"There is an answer to all the questions you kids ask. Let us hurry back and I will explain along the way," Granny told them.

"You already know what is going on, Granny?" Zee asked.

"Well child, you still think there were no evil witches and flying monkeys?" Granny chuckled nervously.

"So, are you saying that there are evil witches and flying monkeys attacking our town!!," Zee asked, half scared, half skeptical.

"No honey, there is someone far worse than both those witches put together," Granny told her in a sad and worried voice.

"What could be worse than flying evil witches that are followed around by flying monkeys," SarCat chimed in "Leader of the Dragon Soldiers; he is a Warlock that has no name. He is the brother of the East and West Witches and his coming to Munchkin town can only mean one thing and it is not good."

"Just tell us, Granny! We believe you now, so please just tell us!" Zee said exasperated, wanting to know what they were up against.

"He has come to kill our KING! He wishes to take vengeance upon Jerry for his part in the killing of his sister the Wicked Witch of the East.

"What part could Jerry have had in that?" Mikey asked.

"Walk quickly, we must hurry," Granny said as she continued to explain King Jerry's role.

With newfound strength at the sight of a figure to shoot at, the General ordered once again, "Take aim! FIRE!" Cannons sounded through the air alongside rifles and other more uniquely fashioned weapons. At the same time, the medallion dangling from the Warlock's neck began to emit a strong luminous glow and a shield enveloped his body protecting him from the onslaught of manmade weaponry. As Warlock confidently made his way towards the town gate, the General frantically cried, "This is useless! Nothing is stopping him! Retreat to our King! We must do everything to protect him!"

Every army soldier quickly turned around and headed to town to take their final stand. The sight of the Munchkin army fleeing in fear made Warlock smirk. He jerked, with ease, the town gates clear out of the ground and slung over his head. Twenty feet high and three feet thick, the Munchkin town wall was built to protect those kept inside. The Warlock sauntered over to the wall and placed both his boney hands upon it and began to speak in an angry tone. "Seventy-five years ago, to this day, my dear sweet sister's life were stolen. Today, I vow to seek revenge upon all the awful little Munchkins and the one they call their King." Shortly after he spoke, bolts of lightning streaked from his hands and penetrated the wall. Slowly, cracks began to ripple through and around the entire wall until they connected with themselves and caused the once sturdy barrier to crumble at his feet. The Warlock stomped through the rubble and entered the town limping, come out, come out, wherever you are."

Time and time again he mocked, "There's no place like home; there's no place like home." When he found not one Munchkin, he was heard angrily muttering to himself, "Just where ARE those nasty little people anyway?"

As Warlock walked down the only road through Munchkin town, he thought it looked like a ghost town. Reaching the center and the great platform, he saw King Jerry and Glinda standing there with looks of determination. The other Munchkins huddled together behind the platform in fear as they watched the scene unfold. As he came closer to the platform, the Munchkin King yelled out "STOP."

"So, you must be Jerry, King of the Munchkins!" Warlock said, his voice oozing with sarcasm. "Don't they call you the Lollipop Kid?"

Swallowing hard the King tried to reply bravely but his fear showed through. "Yes, that is me."

UNTOLD STORY: FROM LOLLIPOP KID TO MUNCHKIN KING

"I have waited patiently for seventy-five years to come here and meet you," Warlock told him.

"Well, how about me? Have you missed me?" Glinda stepped in front of Jerry to protect him and confront Warlock.

"Oh, I have missed you Glinda, it is good to see you again." Warlock smiled.

Off to the side a soldier whispered to the General, "Do they know each other?"

"I do not know but they sure are acting like they are friends." The General responded.

Their attention returned to the platform as Glinda continued, "All small talk aside, I would like to know why you are here?" she demanded.

"This is between him and me," The Warlock pointed to the King.

"I am here to take his life for his hand in the death of my sisters. Revenge must take its course and I am here to make sure it happens!"

"What about MY sister? The Good Witch of the South?!?!" Glinda screamed passionately.

"I do not care about YOUR sister! ONLY MINE!" He replied with heat in his voice.

"If you want to hurt my beloved Munchkins you must go through me!" Glinda defended with confidence.

"If that is how it must be, then I will agree to that!" He retorted with an evil grin and threw in, "But first I brought along a few party crashers to help me ruin this little Freedom Celebration you have going on."

On command the sky flooded with winged creatures he referred to as his "Dragon Soldiers." Each landed next to a Munchkin and stood in a stance ready to attack when ordered to do so. The Munchkins appeared so defenseless and minuscule next to these giant creatures.

"Destroy the town! Eat the Munchkins! Leave the Lollipop Kid and The Good Witch to ME!" Their master ordered them.

"Wait!" yelled Glinda to the Warlock. "Before this party begins may I suggest one rule?"

"Rule?" asked the Warlock. "Whatever are you talking about?"
Glinda continued, "Let nobody die today in this battle.

"WHAT?" The Warlock nearly laughed in disbelief. "That is the most ridiculous thing I have ever heard. Surely, you cannot be serious. Why would I agree to such a thing?" The Warlock questioned.

"Because" Glinda reasoned, "for hundreds of years we have known each other and not one time have I asked anything of you," Glinda said as she winked at him.

Something in his face went soft for only a moment and it quickly hardened again as he replied, "Okay, for one night only you're precious Munchkins are safe."
In shock and disbelief, the Dragon soldiers exchanged puzzled looks. "Guess there's no dinner for us today." One of them disappointedly pointed out. Licking his lips and shaking his head, he sadly looked back at the platform as Glinda was again drew everyone's attention.
"One more thing," Glinda added.
"NOW WHAT?" Warlock snapped.

"Allow me to change into something more suitable!" Glinda zinged back. She waved her wand and cried out, "MY BATTLE OUTFIT, PLEASE!" A puff of smoke surrounded her, and a light flashed from her wand. Slowly the smoke revealed a completely changed Glinda, sporting a magnificent, armored suit made of pure gold that glistened in the setting sun. As beautiful as she was in her pure white dress, she now stood glorious and strong, ready for battle. The outfit included a bow and arrow and a shield embedded with diamonds.

The Warlocks face could not hide his emotions as he stood in complete awe of her, at a loss for words. "Nice outfit, WOW!" The Warlock muttered but regained his composure and instead said with more force, "I hope you fight as well as you look!"

"Oh, I will do my best not to disappoint you, Thank you very much." Glinda said just as sweetly as she did sarcastically.

Meanwhile, the five teenage Munchkins were walking as fast as their legs could carry them to town followed by their faithful four-legged friend, SarCat. Along the trip Granny finished her story of evil witches and how King Jerry and his two friends together trapped and killed the Wicked Witch of the East.
"That is all horrible but what about now? Can the Good Witch Glinda and our Munchkin army stand up against The Warlock and his Dragon soldiers and actually have a chance?" Mikey asked with concern.

"I just do not know; he is so much more powerful than his sisters, the witches." Granny replied gravely.
"What are we going to do," Maria cried.

"We will go home, and we will fight alongside the soldiers; that is what we will do!" Mikey stated with great confidence.

Oh? You heard the old lady. The Warlock cannot be defeated and besides, he has an army of flying Dragon soldiers!" SarCat remarked.
Granny looked down at SarCat walking next to Maria and tried to repay his comment with a kick. SarCat saw her foot coming towards him and quickly jumped out of the way.

"Be nice, SarCat." Maria warned as she bent to pick him up before Granny could try to kick him again. "Why is Warlock so mad? It was a long time ago that his sisters were killed," Maria asked Granny.

"You really have to ask that question," sneered SarCat. "Did you ever consider that it is perhaps because someone dropped a house on one sister's head and the other was melted with a bucket of water?"
Granny looked at SarCat and spoke, "Your cat certainly has a way of putting things, but he is right. Let us pick up the pace," She ordered. Then Granny

began to walk faster in hopes of getting back to town in time to help defend King Jerry, Glinda, and Munchkin town against The Evil Warlock.

CHAPTER 3

WARLOCK V.S. GLINDA

"Destroy this town! Gather the Munchkins together along with their beloved pets." The Warlock ordered, "But don't kill them, I have plans for them after I deal with the last Good Witch and King Jerry." The Dragon soldiers jumped into the air and started to attack the town; every Munchkin started to run for cover. The Warlock turned to look at Glinda and said, "I am sorry for what I am about to do to you!"

Out from Warlock's enflamed red eyes shot a brilliant beam of light aimed directly at Glinda. She raised her shield just in time. The shield reflected the beam at the Warlock hitting him in the chest, the force throwing him backwards into a nearby house, which collapsed on top of him.

"WOW! That was great!" King Jerry shouted as he came around Glinda to get a better view of the fighting. One minute later a roar sounded from under the collapsed house, the house exploded upwards, throwing debris everywhere! Emerging from the wreckage, The Warlock walked towards Glinda saying, "That's not bad," as he wiped the dirt from his black suit. "But you are going to have to do much better than that to beat me!"

Glinda cocked her bow, firing three successive arrows into the Warlocks chest; he stopped, looked down at the arrows, smiling as he pulled them out and then started to walk towards her again.

The Good Witch quickly pointed her magic wand at him, an ice beam shot out from it, hitting The Warlock, and instantly freezing him inside a huge piece of ice. He smirked from inside the ice and suddenly his eyes turned fiery red, and his black suit started to glow like it was on fire. The ice rapidly melted, freeing him from his icy bondage. Still smiling The Warlock again started to

13

walk towards the Good Witch and the King standing on the platform. Glinda readied another arrow but before she could fire, another beam of red light emanating from Warlock's eyes hitting the bow and destroying it, also knocking Glinda to her knees.

The Warlock then raised his hand, pointed at her, saying, "Feel my power!" With his other hand he pointed to a large tree nearby, "You! Come alive and take hold of The Good Witch." The tree came to life. Its roots surfaced from under the wooden stage breaking it in half, the King fell to one side, but the tree roots grabbed Glinda's feet and quickly wrapped around her until she was entombed, only her face could be seen.

The Warlock walked over to where Glinda was being held prisoner by the tree. He affectionately touched one of her earrings and remarked, "I remember when I gave those to you."

"So, do I," answered Glinda in a weak voice.

"You will become one with this tree in three days' time at sunset," stated The Warlock.

Glinda spoke, "You made me a promise, no one will be killed."

"I've killed no one here," The warlock answered. "Now from this day on you will tell everyone that I rule all lands."

"Master, we destroyed the town, and we have every Munchkin along with their pets gathered in one place like you ordered," spoke The General of the Dragon soldiers.

.

The Warlock looked over at him, then at the Munchkins. They were all shaking in fear and shock after seeing their homes in ruins and the defeat of The Good Witch of the North. The Warlock walked over to them and stood in front of them. Two Dragon soldiers came over carrying King Jerry and dropped him in front of their master.

"Well, Jerry, I have been waiting to meet you," sneered The Warlock.

"Oh really? Why?" Jerry asked, but he knew the answer.

The Warlock knelt to look him straight in the eyes, "If it wasn't for you my sister, The Witch of the East, would still be alive."

"That is true! But your sister deserved it, so did her ugly sister The Witch of the West," responded King Jerry proudly.

The Warlock smiled at King Jerry saying, "I was wondering for years what kind of creature could kill an evil witch besides The Good Witches. I know the human girl named Dorothy was one such creature, only she went back home to a place called Kansas. So, that means after I take care of you, my two sisters' will be avenged! Now, what should I do with you and all of the Munchkins?" The Warlock thought out loud.

One of the Dragon soldiers standing beside The Warlock asked, "Master, why can't we eat these Munchkins?"

"I made a deal with Glinda that is why! Warlock shouted.

Another Dragon soldier whispered to the first Dragon soldier, "I think master is getting a heart."

The Warlock turned away from King Jerry; he now walked in front of the Dragon soldier that just whispered the remark. He looked him in the eyes, "So, you think that I am getting a heart?"

"No master!" cried out the soldier, "I didn't mean it!"

"Well, let's just show everyone here how big my heart is!" sneered The Warlock, he then placed his hands on the medallion, it began to glow, The Warlock pointed to him and said, "I'm hungry too, become bite size!" The Dragon soldier screamed as he started to shrink in size until he was only a foot tall. The Warlock reached down, picked him up with one hand and looked him in the eyes, his mouth opened wide showing his teeth. The Warlock raised the soldier over his wide gaping mouth and dropped him inside. The tiny soldier continued to scream as he was swallowed in one gulp, The Warlock let out a long nasty burb saying, "Anyone else think I've got heart?"

"No master!" yelled out every Dragon soldier in unison.

Slowly, he turned back to the Munchkin King, "Now, Jerry, where were we before we got interrupted? I cannot kill you or your people because of that promise, so, let us turn you all into something." Warlock rubbed his chin thinking hard about what to do with the Munchkins. After a few moments he got an evil grin on his face and said, "I got it! You and the rest of the Munchkins will remain here to keep The Good Witch company!" He grabbed his magic medallion, held it over his head and spoke, "I call upon the power of this medallion to grant me revenge on these Munchkins and turn every living pet of theirs into a stone statue."

CHAPTER 4

LAST OF THE MUNCHKINS

Granny, SarCat and the Munchkin teenagers were getting closer to home, when suddenly Puff started to sneeze uncontrollably.

"Oh no, that is not a good sign," spoke SarCat. "I think trouble is coming our way again."

Look up in the sky ahead, there must be over a hundred of those Dragon soldiers and that tornado," cried out Maria.

"Everyone hide again until they pass by," Granny suggested. Everyone dove under some branches and leaves nearby; they remained hiding and quiet until the danger of those Dragon soldiers and the tornado carrying The Warlock passed over. As soon as the winds of the tornado passed Mikey came out.

"It is okay to come out, the danger is gone," he said. Everyone came out from their hiding spot; they all watched the tornado fade away into the distance. "I think we are too late," Mikey said in a worried voice."

"Let's hurry!" Granny shouted. "There still could be Munchkins that need us."

Granny and the others started to run; Munchkin town was only a short distance away. SarCat was running ahead and reached the town before the rest; he stopped and waited until everyone caught up.

"WOW! Look what happened to our town," cried out Maria as she saw the walls of the town destroyed.

"Let's stay together," said Granny with a concerned tone.

"Yea, that's a good idea, you can lead," stated SarCat.

"I'll go first," said Mikey, he climbed over parts of the broken wall and entered the town followed by the rest of the group. There were no signs of life, no sounds of any kind, every house was ripped apart.

Once they reached the end of the main road, they heard a women's voice call out, "Over here!

"Hey, someone is calling for help," Granny yelled. "It is coming from the center of the town square."

They all hurried in the direction of the voice. As they rounded the corner, Mikey could not believe what he saw; every Munchkin including the King was now a stone statue! Granny started to weep after seeing them, Zee gave her a hug saying, "Don't worry, we will find a way to bring them back to life."

SarCat yelled out, "Over here guys." He was standing beside the tallest tree in town looking up at it. Everyone ran over to SarCat, they now saw what he was looking at. Glinda's face was in the center of the tree trunk.

Granny walked up to her, "What happened here my Good Witch?"

Glinda explained how the Warlock came to town to revenge, after she finished telling the story Maria asked, "There must be something we can do to change you back along with our loved ones?"

"Well, there is only one way," Glinda answered Maria.

"What is it!?" Mikey excitedly asked.

"You must somehow get The Warlocks medallion; bring it back to me within three days, but before the sunset of the last day."

"What!" SarCat shouted." That means we must kill that, Warlock."

"Be quiet" Maria said, she picked him up and held his mouth closed.

Glinda spoke again, "I know this is most dangerous, but The Warlock does not know you are alive. I have a plan that may work, but only if we work together."

"Just tell us what we have to do," Mikey spoke up.

"First thing, Granny, please take everyone back to their homes, except for Mikey and Zee, I need to talk to them alone, pack enough food and drinks for three days, and include clothes for hot and very cold weather. One more thing, bring your weapons!!"

"Yes, Glinda," Granny replied, she then turned to the group of teenagers, "You heard the Good Witch, let's get packing." Everyone left while Mikey and Zee stayed behind to hear what Glinda wanted to tell them.

"What did you want to talk to us about?" Zee asked.

Glinda answered, "I need you to go find something to write with, also a piece of paper the size of a map, okay?" "Yes, my good witch," replied Zee. She quickly ran to the nearest house to look for what Glinda asked for.

"Now, as for you my dear Mikey," spoke Glinda. "You are a very clever inventor, the best in all four lands. I know you have been working on a special invention in the basement of your home."

"How did you know about that, I told no one about that!?!" Mikey questioned.

"I am a Good Witch remember," Glinda remarked with a smile. "It is time that you give that invention of yours a test run, get to the basement and have it ready to go by dawns early light."

"I don't know if it is still in one piece," Mikey replied.

"Oh, it is still there!" Glinda answered. "There is one more thing, remember, in the fight that will come with The Warlock the only way to defeat him is from the inside with love, so, please climb up to my face and take one of my earrings with you for luck, when the time comes you will know how to use it."

Mikey listened to Glinda but was puzzled by what she had told him. He did not question her though and did as she requested. Afterwards he put the one earring in his pants pocket. "Now go and get your invention ready." She said with urgency.

"Yes, my Good Witch, as you request!" Mikey replied. As he walked away, he passed Zee on her return to Glinda. "I will see you later," he said as he passed her.

"Okay," She replied. "I am back, I found what you asked for," Zee told Glinda as she stood in front of her holding a large blank piece of paper and a writing stick.

"That's perfect my dear," Glinda told her, "Now, place the paper on the ground and hold the writing stick over the center of it." Zee did as she was told, Glinda closed her eyes and with her mind she took control over Zee's writing hand. Zee's hand started to draw and write on the paper.

"WOW! This is cool, I am drawing a map without thinking about it," Zee said smiling at Glinda. After a few minutes, her hand stopped and released the writing stick. Glinda opened her eyes again; she smiled at Zee, and then looked at the map on the ground.

"Oh, that is perfect," Glinda remarked. "On this trip you will be the map holder, give directions as needed to the one who is driving. Now, take the map with you, go home and pack for the trip and come back here, we will sleep outside here under the full moonlight. Zee did not fully understand what The Good Witch was talking about, but she agreed and returned home to pack for the trip. Glinda looked at the moon slowly rising, the moon beams started to light up the early night sky. Soon Granny, SarCat, Maria, Maven and puff returned carrying their belongings. Granny put her bag besides Glinda's tree saying, "I am sleeping here tonight, and the rest of you find a place to sleep." She then unrolled her bed and climbed in, "Good night, see you all at dawn." The rest of the group sat in a circle and waited for Mikey and Zee to arrive.

About an hour later Zee returned carrying her bag, "Hi everyone," she said, "Where is Mikey?"

Maven answered, "We thought he was with you?!?!"

"Don't worry about him, he is doing something for me; he will be here at dawn," Glinda stated. "Now please, everyone sleep while you can, you won't be getting much of it in the next few days." Everyone did as Glinda asked; they laid down and closed their eyes. They got very little sleep thinking about what had happened that day and what was going to happen in the next few days. Hours later, just before dawn's first rays, the group and Glinda were awakened by a noise coming down the town's only road.

"What is that noise?" SarCat wondered. Everyone watched as the noise came into sight.

"What is that thing?" SarCat asked in a puzzled way.

"It is Mikey," Zee shouted. "Look! He has a ride for us!"

"Whatever he is riding in looks like my old litter box, only bigger," stated SarCat.

Mikey drove his wheeled contraption towards his friends, smiling he said "This is my niftiest invention ever! I call it The Wagon."

"Boy, you sure put a lot of effort into that name, didn't you," SarCat stated sarcastically.

"Oh! Be nice," spoke Maria and picked him up in her arms.

Mikey climbed out to greet everyone, and then they all walked over to Glinda.

"I see you made it, good morning to you, each one of my brave Munchkins," Glinda said cheerfully.

"Good morning!" They replied.

"Now enough small talk, you all must get started on your way to The Warlock's castle, so get into Mikey's wagon and go!" Glinda demanded.

"Okay," answered Granny, speaking for everyone. "We are going, don't worry I will watch over the kids."

Everyone said good-bye to Glinda and climbed into the wagon. There were six seats total in the wagon, one for each Munchkin. After they were in Mikey started it, then mashed his foot down on the pedal, the wagon slowly started to move, everyone waved good-bye to Glinda once more and to all the stone statues, which were their families and pets, that were counting on them.

CHAPTER 5

WE ARE OFF TO SEE THE WARLOCK

"Does anyone know the way to The Warlock's castle? Or do we drive in this thing until The Warlock finds us?" SarCat asked.

"I do!" Zee answered.

"Oh, really my dear," questioned Granny.

"The Good Witch had me draw a map to his castle," Zee pulled out the map from her bag, unrolled it and showed it to everyone.

"WOW! That is great Zee, I am glad you are sitting in front of me! Mikey said excitedly.

"I bet you are," came a cat's voice from one of the seats behind her.

Puff and Maven were sitting in the two-back seats and started to laugh at what SarCat said. Zee just smiled at Mikey, and he smiled back and asked Zee, "Which way do we go?"

Zee looked at the map opened on her lap, "The map shows that we travel due South for half of the day until we come to the desert." Zee rerolled the map and returned it to her bag.

.

"The desert?" Mikey asked.

"That is the first place we must pass through," Zee stated.

"How many places do we have to go through?" Granny asked sitting in the seat behind her.

"I don't know the map only shows one part of the journey at a time," stated Zee. The wagon was made of hardwood, tires were also made of wood, the floor had secret compartments that hid the motor, and some built in inventions. "Hey Mikey, what is all those colored buttons for?" Zee required as she looked at them mounted on the floor between the front two seats.

"Well, each button controls a different kind of invention on the wagon. I had a dream a few months ago and, in that dream, I was inspired to design this wagon along with built in surprises, so I designed the wagon according to the dream I had." Replied Mikey.

The group traveled for hours without seeing anyone; soon they reached the border of the desert. Mikey turned the motor off saying "Everyone out, let's stretch our legs." Everyone climbed out, once they were standing on the ground, they looked at the vast desert before them.

"We have to cross that?" asked Puff as he unwrapped and began to eat one of his Munchkin candy bars.

Zee took out her map again, looking at it said, "Yes, we must cross that, the map tells us to change our clothes for hot weather." She stopped talking then and in a worried tone stated, "The map also tells us to be careful of the Lizard Snakes that live under the sand."

"What are Lizard Snakes?" Maria asked, worried.

"I've got a feeling I am not going to like the answer to that question," remarked SarCat.

Zee continued, "They are over ten feet long, live under the sand, hunt, and eat anyone that travels the desert. The map also warns not to look the in the eyes, they will hypnotize their prey putting them fast to sleep, then eat them whole as they sleep."

"What!" Squealed SarCat, "We got to get past those guys!"

"Don't worry, we'll make it," Maria told him as she started to pet him trying to comfort him.

Granny spoke up, "Girls come with me, and we'll change into something for the hot weather." Zee and Maria followed Granny until they were out of the line of sight of the boys.

"Okay guys let's change while the girls are gone." Mikey stated. After a few minutes, the girls returned wearing cooler clothes, the boys also changed into short pants and short-sleeved shirts.

"Okay guys, we are ready," spoke Granny.

Mikey answered, "We are also, so let's climb aboard and get going," once everyone was back in their seats, Mikey turned to Zee, "let's get this wagon ready for the desert, push in the brown button." Zee looked down; locating the brown button she pushed it. The wagon started to make funny clicking noises, each wooded tire converted into a big fat tire that was perfect for traveling on the desert sand; suddenly a trap door popped open from the center of the floor. A long pole extended upwards, then a full-size tarp unfolded turning into a sail. Mikey checked the tires and sail, and then pushed the motors start button. The wagon soon began to chug onto the desert sand. As it did the wind started to blow filling the tarp with air, helping push the wagon faster.

"Boy! What a great invention," yelled Puff from the back seat.

"Yea, we are really moving now," remarked Maven to Puff sitting next to him.

"I do not think any Lizard Snakes can catch us! Maria remarked to Granny.

"I hope you are right, but I doubt it!" remarked Granny back to Maria as she investigated the open desert. "I think we all should keep our eyes open for any signs of those Lizard Snakes," Granny added.

"Good idea," agreed Mikey. For the next few hours everyone watched the sand for any indication of Lizard Snakes.

CHAPTER 6

BEWARE OF LIZARD SNAKES

The winds began to blow stronger making the wagon move faster and faster. "WOW! It feels like we are about to fly," Zee commented, her long hair blowing in the wind making it hard to see anything.

"Yea, at this speed we should be across the desert before those Lizard Snakes realize we are here," shouted Mikey in a happy tone.

"Everything looks good behind us," shouted Maven from the back seat, he and puff were keeping a close watch out for signs of trouble coming from behind while Granny and Maria sat in front of them watching for trouble coming from the sides of the wagon.

"Yeah, this trip is going to be a piece of cake," shouted Puff while eating another Munchkin bar.

"Is that the only thing you think about," SarCat asked Puff pointing to his Munchkin bar. But before Puff could answer him, he started sneezing. "NO! Not again," SarCat complained loudly. "The last time you did that The Warlock and his Dragon soldiers showed up."

Mikey yelled out, "Trouble coming soon, everyone keep your eyes open!"

It was not long after Mikey spoke that Maven said, "Hey, what is that coming up behind us?"

"I'll give you one guess!" SarCat said as he jumped unto Maria's lap to protect her from approaching danger. Everyone now looked behind them at the desert for the danger that they knew was coming.

"How much longer do we have until we reach the end of the desert?" Mikey asked Zee as she looked at the map again.

"About ten more minutes at this speed," Zee replied. It was not but a few minutes later that the wind stopped, only the wagons' motor kept the wheels turning. The wagon slowed.

"OH NO! We lost the wind power," cried Maria.

"That's not all, there are two of those Lizard Snakes following us and they are gaining," Shouted Maven from the back of the wagon.

"We'll never make it out of this hot desert alive," SarCat said in a hopeless manner.

"Have a little faith in my invention, it won't let us down." Mikey told them all. He then reached down and pushed another button. After he pushed it, the wagon made another creaking sound, the sail and the pole retracted into the trap door, then Mikey told Zee to push the yellow button. Zee reached down and did as Mikey requested, after the button was pushed a trap door popped open in front of each seat exposing a set of foot pedals.

Zee smiled at Mikey and said, "You think of everything."

"I try," he replied with a smile. Now, everyone start pedaling before those things catch us." Everyone did as Mikey directed and soon the wagon moved faster.

"Hey, it's working," shouted Maven, "Those two Lizard Snakes are falling behind us!" Everyone cheered! They all kept on pedaling as fast as their legs could.

Their cheers were short lived and abruptly interrupted when Zee looked ahead and cried, "Oh No, more Lizard Snakes are in front of us."

Granny shouted, "More of them are coming at us from both sides too!"

"We are trapped!" SarCat shouted.

"What are we going to do?" Zee asked Mikey.

Mikey, looking around at all the Lizard Snakes, and then he saw the end of the desert, "Zee, when I tell you, push the blue button, everyone else get your weapons out and get ready to fire them." It only took a minute for the Munchkins to ready their weapons.

After a few more minutes the Lizard Snakes were close enough to the wagon for Maven to launch his arrows. "Fire at them! Mikey ordered. Maven pulled his bow, firing two arrows at one of the Lizard Snakes; the arrows hit their target killing it. Mikey remembered about not looking into their eyes, but before he could warn everyone the Lizard Snakes which were attacking from the sides spotted Maria, Granny and SarCat. They glared right into their eyes. Before they could fire at the Lizard Snakes, each one was in a hypnotic spell and fell into a deep sleep. Mikey saw them fall asleep; quickly he told the others "Reach down under your seats for a pair of sunglasses I put there." They found them and put them on.

Maven shouted, "More of them are coming towards us! If you have any more inventions in this wagon now is the time to use them!"

Mikey looked around the wagon and saw Lizard Snakes closing in on all sides; he knew they had only a mere seconds before they were caught. "Zee push the blue button NOW!" Mikey shouted. Then Mikey instructed everyone to use the straps tied to their seats and to buckle up. "Zee reach behind you and buckle up Granny and Maria and hold SarCat."

"Okay" Zee said and did as instructed. When she was finished, a hidden door opened underneath the wagon, a big built-in compressed spring that was locked in place but ready to be sprung. Mikey asked, "Everyone tied to your seats?"

"YES!" Zee, Maven, and Puff confirmed.

Mikey pulled a rope that was beside him, "Hold on! He yelled. The highly compressed spring shot downward hitting the sand below. The wagon bound up high in the air and as it was climbing Mikey shouted, "Zee, push the white button." As soon as she did the wooden wing popped out from both sides of the center of the wagon. Mikey pulled up on the steering wheel, lifting the wagon up just enough.

The Lizard Snakes tried to grab the wagon with their two front legs that had hands instead of feet, but it was too high for them.

"Maven shoot more arrows at them," Mikey shouted. The Lizard Snakes screamed out in pain after getting hit.

Zee pointed ahead, "It is the end of the desert, we are going to make it!" She then leaned over and kissed Mikey on the cheek. Mikey smiled and turned red. Maven and Puff sang out, "Mikey got a girlfriend, Mikey got a girlfriend."

"OH! Shut up you, guys!" Mikey blushed. "I see and open field, let's land there." He pushed the steering wheel down and the wagon started to lower, crossing over the desert onto the land unknown to any Munchkin. Mikey guided the wagon down to the ground. The fat wheels used for sand popped as they hit the hard ground, the spring compressed itself inside, the trap door closed and locked. Mikey then pushed down on the brake and the wagon slowly stopped in the center of the open field.

UNTOLD STORY: FROM LOLLIPOP KID TO MUNCHKIN KING

SarCat woke up saying, "Are we there yet!"

Mikey smiled and said, "Not yet." Granny and Maria started to wake up. Mikey said, "I think this would be a good time to break for snacks and let Granny and Maria wake up all the way. I also need to check out the wagon for any damage." Everyone slowly climbed out and rejoiced in surviving the Lizard Snakes and desert.

CHAPTER 7

THE WARLOCK CASTLE

Meanwhile, deep underground in The Warlock's castle, The Warlock was enjoying victory over the Good Witch of the North also the satisfaction of getting revenge on the Munchkin King Jerry and his people. All the evil creatures that live in his castle along with The Dragon soldiers were celebrating. They knew in a few days' time everyone that served The Warlock would join him when he moved into the castle above-ground. Warlock was sitting in his favorite chair watching the fire burn in one of the many fireplaces thinking about how he could rule the four lands above-ground when a knock came from the door, "Come in," bellowed Warlock.

The door opened, and two Dragon soldiers slowly walked in towards him, as the pair approached one of them whispered to the other, "You tell master."

"No, you tell him, the second Dragon soldier said nervously.

The Warlock heard those whispers, "What news do you bring me?" He demanded.

Both Dragon soldiers stood in front of in, afraid to tell him the news. One of the soldiers knelt on one knee and said "Master, we have some bad news; one of our spies has just told us that the Lizard Snakes had some trespassers in their desert."

"So, why is that bad news for me?" he asked with a puzzled look.

"Well, the trespassers were Munchkins." The Dragon soldier whispered.

"WHAT!" Yelled Warlock in anger, he stood up throwing his full cup of blood wine into the fireplace. Both soldiers fell backwards and started to shake in fear. "How many are there and where are they now?" The Warlock demanded.

"Master, a total of six still live, we think they were heading toward Snow Tiger Mountain," The Dragon soldiers spat out.

"But how did they get across the desert and pass the Lizard Snakes," he asked getting angrier?

"It was told that they are traveling in a wooden box with wheels that moves fast on land and wings that make it fly,"

The Dragon soldiers told The Warlock. The Warlock heard enough, he grabbed the medallion hanging around his neck, he spoke several evil words then pointed to the Dragon soldier that just gave him the bad news. Instantly he shrunk in size just like the one earlier, then he walked over to him grabbing his tail and swallowing him whole. The remaining Dragon soldier stood shaking in fear thinking he was next. "Don't worry, I won't eat you!" Warlock told him. "He was the one that was dumb enough to tell me bad news, not you."

"Thank you, Master! The Dragon soldier replied still shaking.

"Now, take six Dragon soldiers and go to Snow Tiger Mountain, kill those Munchkins and don't come back with any more bad news!" The Warlock ordered.

"Yes, Master! You can count on me," the soldier answered, he turned away running out of the large room through the castle until he reached the huge front doors. A group of Dragon soldiers were outside standing around when they saw him, one asked, "Why the hurry brother?"

"Master has ordered me to take six soldiers to Snow Tiger Mountain to find and kill a few Munchkins that got away," the Dragon soldier stated.

The group that totaled six smiled at him and said, "We're hungry, let's go!"

"Okay" replied the first soldier, "Follow me!" He then jumped into the air flapping his wings towards the exit of the cave, the group of six happy Dragon soldiers followed hoping to get a bite to eat.

The Warlock started to think, "How could I miss those Munchkins?" Oh well, I am sure my Dragon soldiers will find them soon and that will be the end of Munchkins forever. He walked out of the room still thinking, "Now, why do I have the feeling that I am forgetting something about someone."

CHAPTER 8

SNOW TIGER MOUNTAIN

Back at the open field, the Munchkins and SarCat were enjoying their break eating and talking. "Boy! That was some good food you made Granny," Puff remarked after finishing his third plate.

"It took you three plates of food to figure out that Granny, is a good cook?" SarCat asked.

"Well, I wanted to make sure," Puff replied with a smile. Everyone started to laugh, SarCat just smiled at him not making any more remarks. Zee walked over to Mikey; he was still under the wagon making sure it was still in working order after hitting the ground so hard when they landed.

"Is the wagon alright?" Zee asked Mikey as she bent down looking at him working on something underneath.

Mikey looked at her smiling and answered, "I think so, but we still have a long way to go."

"Well, I know anything that you have invented won't let us down," she smiled.

Mikey came out from underneath the wagon, smiled at Zee, and then said to everyone, "The wagon is ready to go, is everyone done?"

"We are done," Granny spoke for everyone.

"Good, all aboard," Mikey requested jokingly. Within a few minutes everyone was back in their seats and the group was on the move again. "Well Zee, which way does the map say we go next," inquired Mikey.

Zee pulled the map from her bag and after studying it she answered him, "We go there," Zee pointed to a mountain in the distance, "It is called Snow Cat Mountain, and the map tells us once we reach the top we should camp there for the night."

SarCat jumped on her shoulders to see the map, "What else does it say?" He inquired.

"Well, it also warns about Snow Tiger's," Zee replied in a low and worried tone. SarCat jumped onto the map and read the warning aloud, "Snow Tigers inhabit the top of the mountain, they can grow to be eight feet in length, all white with blue eyes and they have razor sharp claws and teeth."

SarCat shrieked "Great, I am going to become cat food!"

"Oh, no you won't," quickly spoke Maria looking at him.

"How do you know that?" he asked as he jumped into her lap.

.

"Because you are going to speak to them and tell them we are friends! Maria told him.

"WHAT! ARE YOU CRAZY? I AM NOT GOING NEAR THOSE THINGS," SarCat shouted at her.

"Well, if you don't then they will surly hurt me," Maria started to cry. One thing that SarCat cannot stand is to see her cry.

"Alright, don't cry," he said as he rubbed against her trying to cheer her up.

Mikey and Zee smiled at each other, they knew Maria was tricking him and not really upset.

Maria looked at SarCat, "Thank you, you are my hero," and gave him a big kiss. Everyone cheered: SarCat! SarCat!"

"Oh, stop it!" He laughed.

For the next hour the group traveled along a pathway that was wide enough for the wagon, it went straight towards Snow Cat Mountain. Once they reached the base of the mountain, Mikey saw a pole stuck in the ground with a sign nailed to it. He stopped the wagon but kept the engine running.

Zee also saw the sign and read it aloud, "Snow Tiger Mountain ahead, enter at your own risk!"

"Oh, I don't like those words," SarCat remarked.

"Well, we are going anyway," Maria told him.

"Let's make a fast change of our clothes here for cold weather," Mikey suggested. Everyone climbed out of the wagon, carrying their bags with them, since there was plenty of trees and bushes around for each Munchkin to change their clothes. After everyone changed, they returned to the wagon and their seats.

"Before we continue, let us eat again, I am hungry," Puff announced.

"That is a good idea, why don't you eat a few sandwiches to make sure you're full," SarCat told him.

Puff looked at him and asked, "Why do you want me to eat until I am full?"

"Well, the more Snow Tigers eat the less they will look at me as a meal," SarCat said sarcastically.

Granny laughed "Boy, that cat is too much sometimes."

"Okay, let's get this wagon ready for the cold and snow," Mikey ordered laughing. He pushed down the red button, a buzzing noise sounded from under the floor; the seats soon started getting warm while small wooden boxes popped up from the floor in front of each seat blowing warm air out.

"WOW! That is another great idea Mikey!" Zee said excitedly as she put her hands in front of the warm air. Then from each tire, tiny wood spikes came out, now the tires could go through any deep snow. Soon the weather started to get colder as the wagon climbed higher towards the top of the mountain.

"Hey, look at those clouds, they look like snow. I hope we make it to the top before the snow starts," Granny stated sounding concerned. Shortly after, the first snowflakes started to fall.

"Hey Mikey, does this wagon come with a top?" Maria asked, as she watched the snowflakes getting bigger.

"Sorry, that is one thing I forgot to install," Mikey replied.

"Oh, that is okay, I like snow," Maria remarked.

"Well, I don't, it is bad for my fur," SarCat complained as the snow started to stick to him. Soon it was getting hard for Mikey to see the path ahead as the wind started to blow with snow. Zee was also looking ahead trying to help him stay on the path.

"Hey look! There is another sign hanging on that tree," Zee pointed out to Mikey. As soon as the wagon was close to the sign Mikey stopped. Zee read it aloud, "STOP! You are now entering the home of the Snow Tigers." Excitedly Zee said, "We made it, we reached the top of the mountain."

"What now?" Puff asked.

"I guess we wait here for something to happen," Granny answered.

"We better keep our eyes open and our weapons ready," Maven said.

Scanning the horizon and seeing nothing but mounds of snowbanks, Zee broke the silence, "I don't see anything but snow, and it doesn't look like anyone is around."

"I strongly disagree; they are out there and watching us right now!" SarCat countered. Minutes later, Puff started to sneeze again. "See, I told you! SarCat remarked in a worried tone. Maven noticed something flying on the horizon below the snow clouds.

"Hey, you guys, look over there in the sky," Maven stated.

Everyone looked, and Maria asked, "What are those things, flying Snow Tigers?"

"Cats can't fly," replied SarCat, "But Dragon soldiers can!"

"Everyone get ready for a fight," Mikey shouted out.

Mikey reached down and pushed the black button. The long pole shot back up from the floor again but this time instead of a sail it took the shape of a large 'Y' that had a large rubber band tied to the top ends making it into a sling shot. Hidden compartments on the sides of the wagon opened and were filled with ball shaped rocks.

Mikey spoke, "Maven and Puff, you guys take charge of the sling shot and fire at those Dragon soldiers when I yell out."

"Okay," both boys answered and prepared the weapon.

Puff told Maven, "I'll be the loader," as he knew Maven was a much better shot than he was. Within minutes, both boys had the sling shot armed and ready to use, while the rest of the Munchkins and SarCat also got ready for the attack to come. Maria took out her weapon from inside her shirt pocket, it was a flute that SarCat made from wood that was given to him by the Good Witch of the North, and she gave the wood magic powers after SarCat finished it. The flute could be used for playing music or be used to shoot out magic darts that sting someone like a bee and knocks them out.

SarCat saw them as they started to fly towards them, "THEY SPOTTED US! He yelled.

CHAPTER 9

SNOW TIGER REVENGE

Flying under the snow clouds the pack leader of the six Dragon soldiers shouted out, "Look boys, it is the Munchkins we have been looking for just ahead.

"Yea, that brown box sticks out in the white snow," said another Dragon soldier.

"Well, boys let's go have some box dinner and don't forget to play with your food before you eat it," ordered the pack leader. The pack of seven started to laugh and dove straight at the Munchkins.

"FIRE!! Mikey yelled. Maven aimed and let go of the rubber band that he pulled back. The rock size ball shot out like a cannon ball straight at the seven flying Dragon soldiers attacking them. The pack leader was flying in front of the others, he saw the ball coming at him and dove out of the way just in time, but the Dragon soldier behind him was not so lucky, the rock hit his head, knocking him out. The Dragon soldier fell helplessly into the snow.

"Great shot! Puff yelled out, "You got one." Then he picked up another rock ball and loaded the sling shot again for Maven.

"Hey, those Munchkins are firing at us!" One of the Dragon soldiers said.

"Watch out!" The pack leader shouted, "They will hit one of us with that long pole, split up and circle the wagon."

The remaining Dragon soldiers quickly flew apart and started coming at the wagon. Maven fired another shot, the rock ball shot out, but this time missed. Puff grabbed another rock ball and was about to load it when he heard, "I don't think so!" The pack leader hit the large pole sling shot breaking it in half, almost knocking the wagon over. Maria, seeing another Dragon soldier attacking from her side of the wagon put her magic flute in her mouth and blew into it. A small dart shot out hitting the flying soldier in his neck. He instantly was knocked out falling into the snow below.

Another Dragon soldier seeing her weapon dove at her, SarCat yelled, "WATCH OUT!" Maria moved to the side as he reached out for her, he missed her but knocked the flute out of her hands into the snow outside the wagon.

"My flute!" Maria said, "It's gone!"

Granny hit another Dragon soldier as he flew by with her walking cane shouting at it, "You won't win this fight!" The pack leader landed in the snow ahead of the wagon blocking it while the rest of the Dragon soldiers landed on all sides of the wagon surrounding them. Zee looked at Mikey, "We're trapped!"

The pack leader yelled to the wagon, "Sorry, that we missed you guys when our master crashed your Munchkins party two nights ago.

Granny stood up angrily shaking her cane at him saying, "Your master turned everyone we love into a stone statue and turned the Good Witch into a living tree, you call that a party!

"Yes, I do!" He replied with a snicker and began to laugh along with the other Dragon soldiers that were standing around the wagon. The two Dragon soldiers that were knocked out slowly started to wake up and soon joined the rest waiting to attack the wagon. Just as the pack leader was about to give the order to attack, something caught his attention. He put his nose up in the air and shouted, "I smell cats!"

The Munchkins looked at SarCat, he looked back at them and said, "Do not look at me! I took a bath before we left."

"Dragon soldiers get ready for a real fight!" The pack leader ordered.

"What is he talking about?" Zee whispered to Mikey. "I don't know but they don't care about us anymore," he answered. The seven Dragon soldiers turned away from the wagon and waited with their weapons out. Soon they saw many pairs of blue eyes popping open looking at them. Their eyes got larger until you could make out the complete silhouettes of the new four-legged visitors. "It's the Snow Tigers," Yelled Mikey as he pointed them out as they ran towards the wagon. The pack leader clenched his fists and pounded his chest repeatedly and gave the order to attack. From the snowbanks jumped out Snow Tigers, but the Dragon soldiers were ready, they fired their net guns hitting them and putting them out of the fight. There was a dozen Snow Tigers that were now attacking the Dragon soldiers, within minutes both groups were in a fight to the death.

"Hey, the Snow Tigers are fighting the Dragon soldiers and not us!" Maria cheered.

"Why?" Puff wondered.

"Because" Granny answered, the Warlock put a curse on them over a hundred years ago and the Snow Tigers seek revenge.

"Who cares why they're fighting as long as they leave us alone," SarCat remarked.

"Should we go help them?" Maria asked. "No, this is a fight between them," Granny replied.

The Munchkins stayed inside the wagon watching as they fought. The Dragon soldiers were stronger than the Snow Tigers and soon started to win the fight between them.

One of the Dragon soldiers approached the pack leader.

"We can't beat all of them." He then pointed to dozens of Snow Tigers running to reinforce their fellow Snow Tigers.

The pack leader looked at them; he knew there was too many Snow Tigers coming to win this fight "Get ready to fly!" He yelled out to the Dragon soldiers still fighting. He turned and looked at one of the Snow Tigers trapped inside the net, "Before we go, I need to get a fur coat for my girlfriend."

The pack leader walked towards the helpless Snow Tiger saying, "You lose!" He then rose up one hand with his claws out and was about to strike it dead when he heard, "LET HER GO!" The pack leader turned and saw a small cat flying towards him, SarCat had jumped out of the wagon and attacked him, and he landed on his back and began to scratch the pack leader in his face and eyes.

"GET OFF ME!" He yelled and tried to get him off.

Maria shouted, "SarCat what are you doing?"

The other Dragon soldiers heard the leaders' screams, and they forgot about the Snow Tigers reinforcements coming. They had all the Snow Tigers tied up and now started to walk over to the pack leader and SarCat fighting, they started to laugh when they saw who was fighting their leader.

SarCat looked behind the Dragon soldiers and yelled out, "Help me cousins!" The six Dragon soldiers turned around and were hit by more Snow Tigers. Now there were dozens of Snow Tigers attacking them. Two more jumped on the back of the pack leader to help SarCat. He looked at them and said, "Hey cousin's nice to meet you!" The two Snow Tigers just smiled at him while attacking the Dragon soldier. SarCat jumps off, letting them fight while helping the Snow Tiger trapped in the net.

The six Dragon soldiers tried to fly away but the Snow Tigers numbers were too much, within a few minutes all six-lay dead, only the pack leader was still alive being held down by four Snow Tigers. The Munchkins stood up cheered after seeing the Dragon soldiers defeated.

SarCat untied the net setting the Snow Tiger free, she stood beside him and said, "Thank you, for saving me, you are my hero."

"Oh, you are welcome cousin," he responded.

Two more Snow Tigers came running up, "Are you okay my Queen," they inquired.

"Yes, Thanks to my brave hero SarCat," she responded with a smile.

"You are the Queen?" SarCat asked.

"Yes, I have been Queen for over a hundred years," She remarked proudly.

"Now, let's go meet your friends in the box with the wheels," she said. SarCat jumped onto the Queen's back, saying, "Lead the way!"

Another Snow Tiger walked over to them and said, "We saved the leader of this pack of Dragon Soldiers for you to question my Queen."

"Thank you, I would love to talk to him," she replied.

The Queen walked over to the pack leader still being held down, she smiled at him and said, "So, your girlfriend wants a fur coat?"

"You'll pay for this!" The pack leader warned.

"The Warlock cursed your people once before; what do you think he is going to do when he finds out what you did here!"

SarCat looked at him and asked, "What does the Warlock know about us?"

"I don't answer to any pet!" The pack leader answered.

SarCat jumped off the Queen and walked right up to his face and said, "If you tell me, I will tell the Queen to let you go."

The pack leader looked over at the six dead Dragon soldiers; he did not wish to join them. "Yes, I will talk. The Warlock knows that six Munchkins and one cat survived his curse on Munchkin town, he sent us here to kill all of you. That is all I know, so, let me go like you promised!"

SarCat smiled at him and said, "I lied!" He then jumped back onto the Queen saying, "he is all yours."

"Thanks," she told him smiling. "My Snow Tigers are hungry for Dragon ribs tonight." The pack leader screamed as he soon met the same fate as the six other Dragon soldiers lying nearby.

The Snow Tiger Queen and SarCat walked over to the wagon, they were soon joined by dozens of Snow Tigers. After they reached the wagon, SarCat jumped off the Queen's back and into Maria's lap saying, "Honey, I'm back!" She gave him a big hug. SarCat said, "Let me do the introductions, Maria, she is my best friend, Granny is old but alright, Maven is a straight shooter, Puff can eat and tell when trouble is coming, Zee is smart, pretty and brave, and last we have Mikey, it is his big size litter box that got us here."

"Hello there! Any friend of SarCat is a friend of all Snow Tigers," said the Queen. "Now, let's get all of you out of this weather and somewhere we can talk, my Snow Tigers will pull your wagon to our hidden cave."

"Thank you, Queen that would be great our wagon needs some repairs," Mikey replied. Within minutes the wagon was tied to six Snow Tigers that led the way back to their home cave.

CHAPTER 10

SNOW TIGER'S CAVE

Meanwhile, back in the underground castle Warlock decided to check on the progress of the seven Dragon soldiers. Inside one of the many rooms in the castle was the seeing well room. He walked into the room and in the center stood a well, it was made of stone and brick, inside the well the water had a special kind of glow to it. The Warlock walks over to it, standing beside it he investigated the glowing water. He took off the medallion from around his neck and held it over the well and spoke the words, "Oh seeing well, show me how my Dragon soldiers are doing." The water in the well began to fog, soon the fog started to show pictures of murdered Dragon soldiers laying in red snow. "What!" Yelled out the Warlock, his voice could be heard throughout the entire castle.

Three Dragon soldiers came running into the room, "Master what has happened?" One asked as they now stood beside him.

The Warlock looked at the three of them and angrily said, "Your brothers have failed to kill the Munchkins!

"How could those little, tiny Munchkins beat our brothers?" They asked in unison.

"They had help from the Snow Tigers," spoke the Warlock as he started to pace around the well thinking about what to do next. The Dragon soldiers watched him without saying a word. After a few minutes Warlock stopped, an evil grin appeared on his face, he turned and walked towards the three Dragon soldiers standing there, "I want NO mistakes this time," he spoke. "You are now a captain, take two dozen soldiers, fly to Snow Tiger Mountain and find those Munchkins also any Snow Tigers and KILL THEM ALL!"

"Yes Master, it will be done!" The new Captain answered. He ran out of the room toward a large pack of soldiers standing in line waiting for Warlock. "ORDERS FROM MASTER! I am the Captain; I need two dozen of you to fly with me now!" The Captain ordered. Within minutes he along with two dozen Dragon soldiers jumped out of many open windows into the air towards Snow Tiger Mountain.

The Warlock looked at the next soldier in line, "I want you to fly to the desert and find the King of the Lizard Snakes, tell him I wish to see him and every Lizard Snake here."

"Yes, Master," he replied, he ran towards the closest open window and dove out following Warlock's order. "YOU!" Spoke the Warlock to the last Dragon soldier.

"Fly to the swarm land and find the Queen of the Puffy Bugs, tell her I wish to talk to her and to bring her swarm of Puffy Bugs along."

"Yes, Master!" He replied and ran jumping out the same open window as the last soldier.

The Warlock thought to himself, "I'm hungry, might as well eat while I am waiting for my guest to arrive." Warlock left the seeing well room and traveled down the long hallway to the cook's room.

Back on Snow Tiger Mountain, the Munchkins and the Snow Tigers had reached a dead end on the side of the mountain.

"Hey, there is a dead end in front of us, where do you think the Snow Queen is leading us?" Zee asked Mikey.

"I don't know but the snow is really coming down, we better take cover soon," he responded.

The Snow Queen stopped right in front of a large boulder and said, "Open says I the Queen!" The large boulder slowly moved to one side, as it did a light showed the hidden cave that the Snow Tigers called home. The Queen entered followed by Snow Tigers and the wagon holding the Munchkins, after everyone was in, the large boulder moved back in place. The cave was large enough for dozens of Snow Tigers to live; it went deep into the side of the mountain with many levels. Once the Snow Tiger's stopped pulling the wagon, the boys quickly untied the knots from the rope releasing it. The Queen came over to the Munchkins saying, "Our cave is your cave. Follow me; I will take you to a warmer room."

"If it is okay with you, I would like to do some repairs to the wagon, Mikey stated.

The Queen answered, "That will be fine, I will have a few Snow Tigers help you, and show you where to find the tools. She ordered two nearby Snow Tigers to stay with the wagon and Mikey. The Munchkins climbed out of the wagon along with SarCat while Mikey stayed behind.

"I will join you after I'm done," Mikey told them as they along with Snow Tiger Queen went into one of the many tunnels. The cave was cold but as the Munchkins went further into the tunnel it opened into a small cave, in the center was a pile of stones that had the reddest glow.

The Queen entered the cave saying, "This will be your room for tonight, and the stones were a gift from the Good Witch of the North. She told us that someday they would warm some new friends. Everyone quickly walked over to the warming stones, except the Queen; she sat close to the cave opening.

"Why don't you join us and get warm?" Maria inquired.

"Because of Warlock's curse," she replied. Get warm my friends, food and drinks will soon be here and when it does, I will tell you the story," the Queen replied. A few minutes later four Snow Tigers came into the cave from another tunnel, strapped to their backs were trays and many mugs of drinks. More Snow Tigers also came in; they had trays of fresh rib. They quickly laid the trays down and left the warm room. Granny put the ribs on top of the stones, they slowly stated to cook.

"WOW! Look at all this food," Puff excitedly commented.

SarCat looked at the ribs now starting to cook and asked, "What kind of ribs are those?"

The Queen smiled at him and said, "Dragon!" Soon each Munchkin along with SarCat were sitting down eating and warming themselves as the Queen started to tell what happened to them a long time ago. The Queen explained how Warlock destroyed their town and turned all her people into large Snow Tigers. She also told them that part of the curse was that if the weather goes above forty degrees, they will die. So, they must not ever leave the cold mountain.

After the Queen told the story, SarCat walked over to her and said, "After we kill that Warlock will that break the curse, he put on you?"

"I don't know how you can, there must be hundreds of Dragon soldiers that live at his underground castle," the Queen remarked.

SarCat smiled back at her and responded, "I have no idea!"

The Queen started to laugh after hearing his response.

Soon the Munchkin joined in the laughter, while Granny yelled out, "Ribs are done!"

Mikey came into the tunnel with another Snow Tiger, "I am done; the wagon is ready to travel at days break." "Good," replied Granny as she handed him a plate of food.

"Thanks," Mikey said as he took the plate and joined his fellow Munchkins.

"The Queen says that we could sleep here tonight," Granny explained to Mikey.

"Thank you! Queen," Mikey said, "We all could use some sleep before we face the Warlock."

"Now, that I told you my entire story, how about telling me why you are going on a suicide mission to the Warlock's castle?" The Queen inquired about the group.

Mikey stood up, "I will be happy to! Our King Jerry helped kill his sister, the Wicked Witch of the East seventy-five years ago."

Zee stood up to continue, "The Dragon soldiers also destroyed out town!"

Maria stood up to add, "He put a curse on our loved ones, turning them into stone statues."

Puff stopped eating to add, "he turned the Good Witch of the North into a living tree."

"WHAT!" The Queen ROARED in anger as she listened to each of them tell her the reason for their mission.

Granny stood up to add, "There is only one chance on beating him, the Good Witch told us how to break his spell and free her and our people."

"How is that?" the Queen asked.

SarCat looked at her and said, "It is simple. We go to his castle, kill him! Take his magic medallion, run for it all the way back to Munchkin town so Glinda can break the spell."

The Queen looked at the group in disbelief after hearing their story and stated, "All of you are brave warriors, I only wish somehow, we could go with you and help you fight that Warlock, but as soon as we leave this cold mountain, we are dead!"

"It is alright cousin!" said SarCat. "We know how you feel about that Warlock and if the Snow Tigers can, they would join us."

The Queen smiled at him, "You guys get some rest tonight, my Snow Tigers will watch over you." Mikey thanked her for all the help. The Queen smiled at him, "You are welcome and thanks for the ribs." She then turned, leaving the Munchkins to sleep. It was not long after they finished eating that they all fell asleep from the long day of traveling and adventure.

CHAPTER 11

ONLY TWO SUNSETS LEFT

After some time, the Captain along with the two dozen Dragon soldiers reached Snow Tiger Mountain and started to search in the darkness for any signs of the Munchkins. A snowstorm was still blowing making it hard for the Dragon soldiers to see even with their keen eyesight at night. "Hey, I think there is something down there," said the Dragon soldier flying next to the Captain.

He looked down, "Yes, I see it, everyone follow me down." Then he lowered his wings and dove down followed by the rest of the Dragon soldiers. Once all the Dragon soldiers landed on the ground, the Captain said, "Everyone keep your eyes open for Snow Tigers." Over a dozen Dragon soldiers were now walking in the deep snow trying to find where the Munchkins were hiding.

After, sometime of searching, One Dragon soldier yelled out, "Over here Captain, I found something."

The Captain ran over to him and seen a long wooden pole that was sticking out of the snow.

"What is it?" asked a Dragon soldier.

The Captain picked it up and looked at it and says, "This must be part of that wagon those Munchkins are traveling in. Our brothers must have had their fight right here."

"Hey, look here, there is blood in the snow," remarked another Dragon soldier walking nearby.

The Captain knelt and smelled the blood, "It is Dragon blood," he growled. So, the rest of the Dragon soldiers came over to see what the Captain found. The Captain stood back up, he looked around at the Dragon soldiers, they were freezing, and everyone left the castle so fast that they forgot to put on snow coats. The Captain also felt his wings starting to ice up, he shouted, "We must leave here now and return to the castle while we can." He then flapped his wings a few times to break the ice from them, he then jumped into the predawn snowstorm followed by two dozen freezing Dragon soldiers. The Captain was not only shaking from the cold but also thinking about what he was going to tell Warlock! The Captain never knew he was a short distance away from the Snow Tigers hidden cave.

Inside the hidden cave the Snow Queen returned to where the Munchkins and SarCat spent the night sleeping. "Good morning Wake up! The sun will be coming up soon," The Queen informed them.

"Good morning, Cousin!" SarCat responded.

The Munchkins slowly started to wake up. Puff was the first to speak, "What's for breakfast?"

SarCat looked at him, "You ate over a dozen ribs last night and you are still hungry?"

"What's your point?" Puff snapped.

The Queen started to laugh, soon two more Snow Tigers came in from another tunnel carrying breakfast for everyone. "Eat my friends, I will meet you at the wagon when all of you are finished, laughed the Queen. She turned back inside the tunnel.

"Okay, thanks again Queen," replied Granny, "We will be there shortly."

The two Dragon soldiers were still flying on the mission that Warlock sent them on. One Dragon soldier was now flying in the middle of the desert looking for Lizard Snakes, "I don't see any signs of Lizard Snakes," he told himself flying high over the desert. The second Dragon soldier reached the swarm lands and began his search for the Queen of the Puffy Bugs and her swarm. Both Dragon soldiers knew that it meant their lives if they did not find them as demanded by their master.

Back inside the Snow Tigers' hidden cave the Munchkins finished their breakfast and walked back to the wagon. The Snow Tiger Queen was waiting with some other Snow Tigers beside it. "How was your breakfast?" Asked the Queen as the group came near.

"It was great!" Puff replied with a smile.

"Yes, thank you for everything you and the rest of the Snow Tigers have done to help." said Granny.

"No, thank you! We have been waiting over a hundred years to pay back the Warlock," The Queen stated.

Mikey looked at everyone, "Let's load up, we still have a long way to go and only two days left to do it."

Once everyone climbed in the wagon, the Queen stood in front of the boulder, "Open in the name of the Queen." Slowly the large boulder moved to the side, reopening the hidden cave. The snowstorm had stopped, and the sun was starting to rise. Mikey started the wagon and it started to move out of the cave.

"Good-bye my friends, I wish we could join you," spoke the Queen.

"Me too cousin," remarked SarCat.

The Munchkins yelled good-bye to her and the rest of the Snow Tigers as they drove away. As they did, a Snow Tiger went to the wagon and handed Maria her flute, "You may need this!"

Maria thanked him saying, "I think I may."

"Hey, Zee take a look at the map and tell me which way we should be going," Mikey asked.

Zee looked at the map and studied it, "We should be close to the top of the mountain soon then we slide down the other side until we hit the stream below," she stated to Mikey.

Once the wagon reached the top of Snow Tiger Mountain, Mikey stopped the wagon and looked at the path ahead, "WOW! Everyone look the other side of the mountain slopes down greatly with only a small path wide enough for the wagon." On both sides of the path were large trees and boulders hitting them could be deadly, Mikey thought to himself.

"How are we going to get down there, it is too steep!" SarCat said nervously.

"We'll make it," Mikey assured him. "Hey, Puff and Maven, give me a hand with the wheels." Mikey jumped out of the wagon along with the boys.

"What's your idea?" Maven asked Mikey.

Mikey reached down under the wagon and pulled out four short skis,' "Help me snap these on the wheels."

The boys smiled at Mikey, "We got your idea now!

After a short time, the boys had put one ski on each wheel, turning the wagon into a sled.

"Hey guys, what are you about to do?" SarCat asked.

"Oh, you'll find out in a minute," Puff answered smiling at him.

"Okay, guys get behind the wagon and get ready to push and when I say jump in do it fast," Mikey explained. The three boys put their hands on the backside of the wagon, "Start pushing," Mikey shouted. The boys pushed the wagon; slowly it began to slide on the snow just before it went over the edge. Mikey shouted, "NOW, JUMP IN!!" They all jumped in the wagon and Mikey made his way quickly to the front seat and grabbed the steering wheel while Puff and Maven returned to their seats. The wagon slowly tipped over the edge, "Hold on!" Mikey shouted and pointed the front wheels toward the open path in front of him. The front skis hit the snow then the back ones, the wagon took off down the side of the mountain.

"WEE!" Shouted Granny, "I haven't been snow skiing since I was a young girl."

"You were young once?" SarCat asked sarcastically.

"Watch it cat!" Granny scolded him.

Soon everyone was holding on tight to their seats while Mikey held onto the steering wheel trying to keep the wagon from hitting the trees and boulders on the sides.

While the Munchkins and SarCat were sledding down the mountain, the Dragon soldiers that were searching the desert for Lizard snakes, spotted something in the sand. He flew lower to get a better view and said to himself, "Those are Lizard Snake tracks." he followed the tracks for miles until they ended at a large looking sinkhole with many Lizard Snakes coming and going from it. The Dragon soldier landed on a pile of large stones near the sinkhole.

It was not long after he was there, when a few Lizard Snakes came over to him and asked, "What brings the Warlock's Dragon soldier to our home?"

"My master ordered me to give your King a message," The Dragon soldier answered.

"The King is gone and won't be back until tonight," replied the Lizard Snake.

The Dragon soldier knew he must deliver the Warlock's message personally and said, "If it is okay with you, I'll wait here until the King returns."

"Any Dragon soldier is most welcome; we will tell the

King you are waiting for him when he returns." the Lizard Snakes stated. The two Lizard Snakes returned to the sink hole, disappearing into the sand and back home to their nest.

The Dragon soldier sat down and said to himself, "I'm tired of flying; I'll just rest here and get some sleep and sun until the King returns."

At the same time back at the other side of Snow Tiger Mountain, the wagon was making great time skiing down the Mountain side. Mikey had both hands on the steering wheel trying to keep the wagon from going off the path and crashing into the trees or boulders, which lined the pathway all the way down the side of the mountain. The rest of the Munchkins were cheering with the excitement as they were skiing down the mountain, except SarCat, his tail was puffed straight out, and his claws were stuck into the wooden sides of the wagon.

"When is this ride going to end, we have been skiing for hours," SarCat shouted.

Zee looked ahead and shouted, "Oh, I think this ride will be ending really soon." Zee pointed ahead, "Look the snow ends and a river starts there."

"What!" SarCat shouted, "We have to go in the water now? I do not like that idea at all, we will sink like a rock."

"Don't be a scaredy cat!" Maria told him. Mikey's wagon invention has not let us down yet."

"I know that but there is always a first time," SarCat yelled back at her.

Mikey asked Zee, "Get ready to pull out the yellow button." Zee reached down and grabbed and held the button and waited for Mikey's order.

CHAPTER 12

KILLER FLYING BUGS

"Zee pull out the yellow button now! Mikey shouted.

Zee pulled the button so hard it came out in her hand, "Sorry about that," she told Mikey.

The wagon made a popping noise then all four wheels fell off just as the snow ended and the water began. The wagon made a big splash as it hit the water; the force stuck everyone in their seats as if they were strapped in.

"WOW!" What a ride," Mikey laughed.

"Great driving," shouted Maven from the back.

"The temperature feels like it is summertime now," Granny remarked. She then took off her snow coat and sat down in her seat. Soon each Munchkin did the same as Granny.

Mikey then pulled out the orange button, instantly from behind the back of the wagon, another trap door opened and enclosed was a small paddle wheel. Soon after that the foot pedals popped open again from the floor, the wagon was now floating. Mikey quickly used the steering as a boat rudder to drive the wagon.

"WOW! This is great." Zee remarked, "Your invention is now a boat!!"

"Yea, it is too bad we don't have any fishing poles, I still like to try some fishing," remarked Maven.

"Look under your seats guys," Mikey told them.

Puff looked and pulled out two fishing poles, "Boy Mikey, you do think of everything!"

SarCat climbed over the seat, joined the boys, and said, "I would like one of you boys to catch me a big catfish."

"We will try," Maven replied. SarCat just sat and watched as the boys put their fishing lines into the water and start to fish.

"If you girls want to, you can use the foot pedals, it will help spin the wheel." Mikey said.

"Okay, we can do that while the boys catch us some fish for lunch," said Granny. So, Granny and Maria put their feet on the foot pedals and started to paddle, the small paddle wheel spun making the wagon move faster in the water.

"Hey Zee, now that we made it past Snow Tiger Mountain, where does the map show we go next," asked Mikey.

"Zee took out the map and studied it, saying, "We take this river into the swamp until it empties into a big lake, once there you will see a small island in the center." Zee stopped and started to read the rest to herself.

"What else does the map show?" Mikey wanted to know.

"Well, we should keep our eyes open for killer flying bugs in the swamp, also AilSharks in the lake" she told Mikey.

SarCat turned around and looked at Zee, "I know I'm going to hate myself for asking this but what are killer flying bugs and AilSharks?"

"Do you really want me to answer that?" Zee remarked.

"No! I do not think so," SarCat replied and turned back around to watch the boys' fish.

"Well, I want to know," Mikey said.

"Okay, I will tell you, the map says that the swamp is filled with many things that bite and sting, but the swarm of flying bugs are the deadliest. They can grow to be four feet round with a long stinger that has enough poison to kill anything with one sting, they are very protective of their Queen and will attack anyone that comes near their nest," Zee responded to Mikey.

"Well, Let's hope we don't run into them," Mikey quickly responded.

"Oh, you all know that we will!" SarCat commented sarcastically.

"Anything else we should know about," Mikey asked Zee.

"Yes, when we make it to the lake, I will tell you then, Okay?" Zee responded. Mikey looked at her in a puzzling way, "Okay!?!"

Zee rolled the map up and put it back inside her pants pocket without saying anymore. "Hey! I have a bite," Shouted Puff as his fishing line pulled him.

SarCat yelled to him, "don't lose him, I'm hungry for some fish."

"I've got a fish on my line too!" Maven shouted.

Puff pulled in a fish saying, "This one is for you SarCat!"

"That is not a catfish" remarked SarCat after looking at it.

"So, what does that mean?" Puff questioned as he unhooked the fish putting it into a bucket of water.

"I'm a cat, so, catch me a catfish Puffy boy," SarCat stated seriously with a bit of humor.

"Oh, that makes sense to me," Puff replied to him. "I'll try harder next time," he said as he baited the hook again and for the next few hours the boys fished in peace while the wagon made its way deeper into the swamp.

Mikey kept the wagon in the middle of the small river to avoid getting stuck in the mud, trees and logs that lined the riverbanks.

"Hey Mikey, I think we have caught enough fish for a late lunch," Maven stated.

"I am still waiting on someone to catch me a catfish!" SarCat reminded the two boys of fishing. It was long a time later when Puff hooked another fish, SarCat watched as he pulled the line out of the water.

"It's a catfish!" SarCat shouted.

Puff smiled at SarCat, "Is this fish good enough for you?"

"Yes, that is a catfish!" SarCat smiled, "Now all we have to do is cook them."

Zee looked at the map again and said, "Around the next bend should be a place we can pull over and make a fire."

Mikey replied, "That sounds good to me." Soon the wagon made its way around the bend.

"Look over there," remarked Zee as she pointed to a clear spot just ahead.

"I see it," Mikey answered. Just as he was about to turn the wagon towards the spot, Puff started sneezing.

.

"Oh No! Not now, we are about to have a fish fry," shouted SarCat.

"I have a feeling we are not going to have time to stop here," Mikey announced to everyone.

"I think we better put the fishing poles away and replace them with our weapons," Maven told Puff as he continued to sneeze.

Granny added, "I think we all better get ready for the danger."

A little while later SarCat said, "I hear buzzing sounds coming from those trees ahead.

Mikey quickly pulled out a small pair of looking glasses that could see things far away. He looked at the tree SarCat was talking about. "It is a large nest of some kind with big bugs, there must be over a hundred of them swarming," Mikey said in a worried voice.

"How are we going to get pass them?" Zee asked.

"We have no choice; we must go forward and fight them off," Mikey stated. Mikey looked at the nest, it was hanging on a large branch that was about fifty feet up from the river. He soon thought of a battle plan. "Okay," he said, "This is what we do, first, we all start paddling as fast as we can to get past that nest, then we fire our weapons in front of our wagon to make a pathway, so we can get by them."

"Okay," spoke Granny.

It was not long before each Munchkin had a weapon in hand and aiming straight ahead of the wagon. One flying bug heard the wagon paddle wheel splashing in the water and flew towards them. Mikey watched him get closer and said, "Maven use your arrow on this one." Maven aimed his arrow at him and fired, the arrow shot straight and hit the flying bug, as it did the bug popped like a firecracker and fell splashing into the water. The sound set out an alarm throughout the flying bug's nest. Within minutes the swarm was flying towards the wagon, this time they were flying with their long poisonous stingers out.

"Get ready, here they come!" Mikey shouted.

"I sure hope you're wagon has another weapon against that swarm of killer bugs coming at us!" SarCat said, now sitting between Mikey and Zee.

"Now that you mention it," Mikey replied. "I have something." Mikey waited until the swarm was about fifty feet ahead and then Mikey yelled. "Take this!" Mikey pulled on the purple button just under his seat, suddenly one hollow three-foot-long pipe pointed out from the front of the wagon to make a homemade cannon. At the same time, foot pedals stopped spinning the paddle wheel; they were now being used as a power source for firing small ball shape items. Within a few minutes a line of five balls shot out of the cannon hitting the water just in front of the swarm, when they hit, they popped open making a thick and stinky cloud of smoke making a fog bank. The Queen of the killer bugs few into the fog first, closely followed by the swarm. The stink was so bad it made the Queen, and her swarms forget about attacking the floating wagon. Mikey shouted, "Now fire into the fog!" From the back seats, Maven and Puff fired their weapons; first Puff used his sling shot firing hand size rocks while

Maven used his bow and arrows. The rocks and arrows flew straight in front of the wagon making a pathway. Firecrackers sounds could be heard from inside the fog as flying killer bugs were being hit, popping, and falling into the water. The Queen killer bug was confused in the fog; she was flying in circles and lost along with her swarm. The wagon slowly floated into the fog.

Mikey gave another order, "Everyone, hold your breath while we go into the fog and defend our wagon."

Granny raised her walking cane into the air like a baseball bat, yelling "COME ON! Send me a fast ball."

SarCat looked at her, "I think Granny is going crazy!"

Maria took out her magic flute and aimed at one of the flying killer bugs coming toward her side of the wagon, her dart shot out straight hitting its intended target, knotting the killer bug, and slapping it into the water. Granny hit two killer bugs with one swing as they flew by.

SarCat yelled, "HOME RUN!"

The Queen had enough of this fight and flew straight up out of the fog and signaled her swarm to give up the attack and return to their home nest. The wagon floated out of the fog, as it did everyone took a deep breath then cheered as they watched the swarm fly away. "We made it; we are safe now!" Mikey announced. He then pushed the purple button back in, the pipe retreated into its original position and the foot pedals started to spin the paddle wheel again.

Zee looked at the map again and said, "Once we go around the next bend in the river, we will enter the big lake and the home of the AilSharks."

"What are AilSharks?" asked Maria.

"The maps shows an island with a large stone shaped fin in the center of the lake, it also gives orders saying that once we reach the island, one member of the group is to walk to the stone fin and knock three times and wait for an answer," Zee continued reading, "The island is the home of the AilSharks! If we wish to cross the big lake, we must ask for their permission," Zee finished.

"I'm waiting to hear what they look like," Maria stated.

'Okay, I will tell you," answered Zee. "They can grow to be eight feet from head to tail, live in and out of water, have the body of a shark and the head of an Alligator with over one hundred teeth!"

"Oh! Those guys sound like a lot of fun," remarked SarCat.

"Well, I guess we will find out once we meet them," answered Zee. The wagon moved quickly as the paddle wheel turned in the water with the help of the foot pedals and was soon past the bend in the river.

"Boy! That is a big lake," Zee remarked as she saw the size of the lake as they left the swamp river.

"I never saw so much water before." remarked Granny.

"How are we ever going to find the island out there?" asked Maria.

"We'll find it," answered Mikey. "We just need to paddle until we see a large stone sized fin."

"I'll play my flute to help pass the time," Maria offered. She took out her flute and started to play while everyone listened and pedaled their way to the island of the AilSharks.

CHAPTER 13

BROTHER, WHERE HAVE YOU BEEN?

Meanwhile, back in Munchkin town, the sun was high in the sky. Glinda looked at the sun thinking; "It has been over two days since they left, I hope everything is going well for my beloved Munchkins." Suddenly, a blue color star came shooting down from the sky and landed a few feet away from her. Glinda smiled as she watched it change into her brother, the Real Wizard of OZ. "It is about time you showed up," Glinda stated.

"I am sorry my sister, I just heard the news," the Wizard of OZ replied. The Good Wizard of OZ, how he liked to be called, Good Wiz was a handsome man wearing a white suit, top hat with a golden pocket watch with a chain attached to the inside of his belt. "Sister what happened to you?" Good Wiz asked as he walked closer to see her face inside the tree trunk.

"The Warlock came back here and did what you see here now!" Glinda answered.

"What? That stuff that happened over seventy-five years ago?" Good Wiz questioned.

"We both know my brother that time doesn't matter to him; he seeks revenge of the deaths of both evil witches.

from the East and the West." Glinda responded and continued, "The Warlock was too powerful for me, he cursed me to live forever as a tree and turned my beloved Munchkins into stone statues, except a few, tough Granny, a handful of teenagers and a sarcastic cat! They were out of town during the attack."

Good Wiz looked around not seeing them and asked, "Where are they?"

"I sent them on a mission," Glinda answered.

"Should I ask what kind of mission you sent them on?" Good Wiz asked.

"Well, the Warlock made one mistake, he didn't get all of the Munchkins and the curse takes three days to fully take place, so they all volunteered to go to his underground castle to get his magic medallion within three days' time so I can break the curse on the Munchkins and myself." Glinda explained.

"Let me try my power to break his curse," announced Good Wiz. He pulled out his golden pocket watch and held it high saying, "Let this evil curse bestowed upon all here be broken and all return as before the Warlock came to town." The pocket watch began to glow and spin at the same time. A bright flash came from the watch going throughout the town of Munchkin. "I don't believe it," remarked Good Wiz, "Nothing is happening! My magic watch has never failed me before."

"I had a feeling that the Warlock's curse was unbreakable by you, so don't feel bad my brother, which is why I came up with a backup plan to break the curse, also a way to defeat him like his two sisters." Glinda explained to him.

Good Wiz put his magic watch back in his pocket and asked, "What is your plan sister and what can I do to help?"

"I am glad you asked," Glinda answered and started to explain her idea while her brother listened closely. "The Munchkins need your help; I want you to visit your friends the Snow Tiger Queen and the King of the AilSharks. Tell them we need their help in the battle that will take place tomorrow."

"So, what else can I do?" Good Wiz inquired.

"Meet the Munchkins at the underground warlock castle and find Mikey; he has the piece of the puzzle that will destroy the Warlock." Glinda replied.

"Oh?" Good Wiz questioned.

Glinda continued to explain the plan to her brother and after she finished, he said, "Boy! That is the plan, I will do my part. I am looking forward to our rematch and this time he will not get away!" Good Wiz pledged to her.

"Oh, brother that was over two hundred years ago and both of you were in high school," Glinda remarked.

Good Wiz smiled at her then kissed her saying, "It is time for me to fly." He took two steps back and turned into a blue star shaped light and flew upward towards Snow Tiger Mountain. The Good Witch of the North could only hope the brave Munchkins were still safe and everything was going as planned.

CHAPTER 14

AILSHARK ISLAND

The Munchkins were still pedaling across the big lake looking for an island with a large fin. "We have been looking for hours and there is no sign of an island anywhere," spoke Maria.

"Don't worry, the map shows that we should be near the island soon," answered Zee.

A few minutes later Granny pointed straight ahead with her cane and shouted out, "Look, it is a fin sticking out of the water!" Everyone looked and just in site was a small, shaped fin coming out of the water.

"Ok" Mikey said, "That must be the island we have been searching for." He grabbed the steering wheel and pointed the wagon in the direction of the fin. As the wagon drew closer the fin grew larger and now a small island could be seen. It was a long time before the wagon reached the island. Mikey spotted a boat dock and aimed the wagon towards it. "We will tie the wagon up to the docks and see what is on the island," Mikey stated.

"Good that means we can cook some fish now." SarCat said hungrily.

"Soon as we make sure the AilSharks are friendly," Mikey replied to SarCat, then ordered, "Everyone stop pedaling. We will coast up to the dock."

"It is about time," Puff remarked, "my legs were getting tired!"

"Mine too," replied Maria.

Once the wagon reached the dock Mikey grabbed a rope and tied one end to the wagon and the other end to the dock, locking it in place. "Alright, I will go and knock three times on that stone fin like the map says to do," Mikey said.

"NO!" spoke Zee, "This job is mine alone to do! You stay here and watch out for danger and let me know when it comes."

"What! I am not going to let you go out there alone!" Mikey said in a very worried voice.

Granny put her hand on Mikey's shoulder and said, "My granddaughter will be fine, let her do what she needs to do."

Mikey looked at Granny then at Zee and said, "If that is what you want, I won't stop you but that doesn't mean I like the idea."

"Thank you, Mikey," Zee replied and gave him a hug and a kiss on the chin.

"WOW! He gets a kiss just for staying in the wagon," SarCat laughed.

Zee climbed out of the wagon and onto the dock, she looked all around, not seeing anyone or thing she started to run towards the large stone fin that was about a hundred feet up the island's beach. Mikey watched and said, "Everyone keep your eyes on her." Zee was at the stone shaped fin, it was tall, almost fifty feet and about ten feet wide, and part of it was buried deep into the sand.

"She is almost there!" Granny shouted as she looked at Zee.

"Uh, oh" Puff shouted.

"What is the matter," SarCat asked in a worried way.

"Achoo, Achoo!" Puff started to sneeze.

"Oh No! I knew it! Danger is coming our way! SarCat shouted.

Everyone started looking at the island, but there were no signs of anyone or anything. "I don't see what is making you sneeze," Mikey commented.

"I don't know why I am sneezing, but it can't be good," Puff replied.

The two dozen Dragon soldiers and the Captain were lost and flying over a big lake when one of the flying Dragon soldiers said, "There is an island down below, let's rest a while."

The Captain looked down and said, "hey, what is that thing floating near the docks?" Oh, it is the Munchkins!" The Captain said smiling then shouted, "It is time boys, let's get them!"

"I know what is making Puff sneeze," SarCat announced.

"What?" Mikey said looking at him.

SarCat raised one paw upwards to the sky and said, "That is the reason!"

Mikey and the rest of the Munchkins looked upwards, and Maria screamed "Dragon Soldiers!!!"

Mikey gave an order, "Everyone get out of this wagon, we are sitting ducks in here, run to where Zee has gone." It only took a minute for everyone to get out of the wagon with their weapons and start running towards Zee.

Zee was unaware of what was happening behind her at the dock, she reached the large, shaped fin and knocked three times like the map said to do. "Hello in there! Is anyone home," she asked. Then she heard voices coming from behind her.

"Zee, take cover, the Dragon soldiers are after us!" Mikey shouted at her.

Zee turned and saw all her friends running up the beach towards her and dozens of flying Dragon soldiers in the air behind them, "Leave that Munchkin girl for me, the rest of you can have the others!" Remarked the Captain Dragon Soldier.

Mikey seen how far away Zee was and knew he and the others could not reach her in time, "Quick everyone make a circle and use your weapons to fight off those Dragon soldiers."

The Munchkins stopped running and made a small circle and aimed their weapons at the oncoming Dragon soldiers.

"Fire!!" Mikey yelled. Everyone shot their weapons at the pack of Dragon soldiers.

"Watch out!" The Captain shouted as he saw the Munchkins arrows, darts and rocks coming from the Munchkins weapons. He turned his wing just in time to avoid the oncoming danger. The three soldiers flying behind him did not have enough time to get out of the way and were hit, falling to the beach below. The rest of the pack divided in half and started flying around the Munchkins waiting to attack. Zee was unarmed and could do nothing but watch, then she screamed as the Captain landed beside her and said, "Hello there, how are you doing?"

Mikey heard Zee scream, he turned to see a Dragon soldier holding Zee up with one hand. "Lower your weapons or I will kill this girl!" The Captain yelled. Everyone heard his command, dropped their weapons, and put their hands up. Mikey yelled, "We give up, please let her go!"

The Captain smiled and released Zee, she dropped to the sand and ran over to the rest of the Munchkins. The rest of the flying Dragon soldiers landed around the group of Munchkins still in a circle, surrounding them. The Captain walked slowly over to the Munchkins and stopped in front of them, "So, there you are!"

The Captain spoke to the group of Munchkins, "I can't believe we found you, our master will be pleased after I tell him that you are dead and eaten."

SarCat whispered to Mikey, "Let me handle this." He then jumped out in front of all the Munchkins and stood just a few feet from the Captain, "I can speak on behalf of my friends behind me." SarCat said in a defiant tone.

The Captain and the rest of the Dragon soldiers started to laugh aloud after hearing SarCat speak. SarCat had noticed something that no one else did. In the calm waters dozens of fins were sticking out and coming towards the beach behind the Dragon soldiers. SarCat was stalling for time.

"That is funny cat," the Captain responded, "But we have nothing to talk about, somehow, we missed all of you in Munchkin town and you defeated our brothers at Snow Tiger Mountain, but your luck ends now!

SarCat started to laugh, while the Dragon soldiers stopped their laughing and looked at him with a puzzled look. "What is so funny cat?" The Captain angrily asked.

"You guys are just as dumb as the Dragon soldiers we met the other day and look what happened to them." SarCat laughed.

"Oh really? How is that?" The Captain asked.

"Well, your brothers talked too much and didn't see what was coming up from behind them," SarCat chuckled.

The Captain thought about what he said, he then turned his head around to check and he yelled out, "OH NO!" Over fifty AilSharks shot out from the lake and the first wave hit each of the two dozen Dragon soldiers circling the Munchkins.

SarCat jumped back inside the Munchkins circle and said, "My work is done, let them fight it out."

Within minutes, AilSharks and Dragon soldiers were in battle on the beach. The AilSharks were close to the Dragon soldier's size from their fin tail to their alligator heads; they could swim in water and walk on land with their long arms with fin claws. The Dragon soldiers were stronger, but they were outnumbered four to one. Shortly after the battle begin it was over and all the Dragon soldiers were dead except for the Captain, he was being held down by five AilSharks moaning in pain from his wound. Additional AilSharks came out at this time, they walked over to the Munchkins and stood beside them, suddenly a loud bang sounded from the large stone fin the Zee had knocked on earlier. The

AilSharks stopped what they were doing and stood at attention, except the five still holding down the Captain. A large door opened from inside the stone shaped fin, out stepped the King of the AilSharks. He was robed in a brilliant red satin cloth with white and black pearls sewn across the front of it. The King walked over towards the Munchkins that were still standing in a circle waiting for all the fighting to end. The AilSharks lowered their heads and raised their tails in respect to the King walking by them. He stopped in front of the Munchkins and asked, "Who knocked on my door?"

Zee took a step forward and answered, "I did, my name is, Zee."

"Well, hello my dear, I am the King of all AilSharks, and we welcome you to our island. How can I help you?"

"Thank you, King, I would like to introduce my friends to you, our leader is Mikey, and the other two boys are Maven and Puff."

The boys said, "Hello King," and lowered their heads in respect.

Zee continued, "The girls are Granny and Maria."

Both girls lowered their heads like the boys did saying, "Hello King!"

SarCat jumped in front of Zee saying, "And finally there is me! SarCat is the name. How are you doing King?"

The King smiled at all of them saying, "It is nice to meet you, we have been waiting for you. But before we talk anymore, I need to say Hello to that Dragon soldier over there." The King turned and walked over to the Captain and said, "You made a big mistake landing on my island."

"Let me go!" The Captain demanded.

"I give the orders around here Dragon soldier," remarked the King. "Now tell me, why are you after those Munchkins?"

"The Warlock will seek revenge on every one of you just like he did to the town of Munchkins!" The Captain shouted.

"What did he do?" the King inquired.

"I will tell you what Warlock did," spoke Zee. "He turned every Munchkin along with their pets into stone statues and then turned the Good Witch of the North into a tree."

"WHAT!" Screamed the King; "Our beloved Glinda was attacked along with those peaceful Munchkins? I heard enough, KILL HIM!" The King ordered. Then he walked away to return to where the Munchkins were still waiting. A loud scream could be heard coming from the Captain as five AilSharks attacked him, tearing him apart.

Once the King reached the Munchkins, he put his hand fin on Zee's shoulder and said, "Any friend of Glinda's is a friend to me, now all of you follow me to a place we can talk and can't be seen by anymore Dragon soldiers." The King yelled out, "Hide that wooden thing tied to the dock and get rid of those dead bodies, leave no trace of them." The King walked back towards the large door inside the fin. Zee followed behind him along with the rest of the Munchkins and SarCat in a single line. Once everyone walked inside the large stone shaped fin, the door closed behind him. The inside of the fin was much bigger than the outside looked. It had a total of six levels, three above ground and three underground. Each level had many rooms that could hold dozens of AilSharks. In the center of the main room was the King's chair, he walked over to it and sat down saying, "Please sit and rest."

The Munchkins did as the King asked, within minutes AilSharks came into the room bringing trays of food and drinks. "Now, tell me," said the King, "How can we help you break the spell the Warlock bestowed on your people and the Good Witch of the North."

Mikey spoke up, "Well, first thing we need is a place to sleep tonight."

"Alright, anything else?" The King asked.

"How about coming with us to the Warlock's castle and fighting those Dragon soldiers of his," remarked SarCat.

The King said, "We would love to join you, but the Warlock cursed us hundreds of years ago, turning us into the creatures that are in front of you now and part of his curse was that we could only live on this island and in the lake and if we leave and travel more than one mile from this island we die!"

"I am sorry to hear that," Mikey remarked sadly to the King. "Some way, somehow, we will find a way to break the Warlock's curse on the Munchkins, the Good Witch of the North and the AilSharks!"

The King smiled at Mikey saying, "Thank you for thinking of us, now sit back and relax while our band plays some songs to celebrate our new friends the Munchkins!" A group of five AilSharks came into the room carrying musical instruments and started to play a song in front of the King and the Munchkins. The Munchkins looked at each other in amazement.

UNTOLD STORY: FROM LOLLIPOP KID TO MUNCHKIN KING

Granny spoke to the group, "Well, let's join the party, shall we?" She walked over to the King and asked, "May I have this dance?"

The King stood up and answered, "It would be my honor." He took Granny's hand and started to dance with her.

Mikey watched them and then asked Zee, "Would you like to dance?"

"I thought you would never ask," remarked Zee. She grabbed Mikey's hand and soon both were dancing beside the King and Granny. The rest of the Munchkins and SarCat watched and enjoyed them.

The band played for hours until the King spoke, "It is time you Munchkins get some rest before the sun rises." The band stopped playing, said good night to each Munchkin and wished them the best of luck tomorrow. The King ordered one of the AilSharks to take all of them to a nearby room to sleep. He then told them, "Sleep in peace and we will wake you up just before dawn."

"Thank you for everything," Granny told the King and hugged him as they were leaving the room on their way to the sleeping room.

After a few hours' sleep the King came into the room where all the Munchkins and SarCat were still sleeping. "Wake up my friends, dawn will be here shortly," said the King in a soft tone.

Granny was the first to open her eyes, "Good Morning King." The rest of the Munchkins slowly woke up.

"When you all wake up, come back to the main room and have some breakfast," spoke the King.

"Thank you," responded Granny, "We will be there in a few minutes."

The King smiled and turned around to let them wake up and left the room to wait for them in the main area. About ten minutes later, all the Munchkins were up and came walking into the main room. There was a table set up filled with all kinds of food and drink.

"WOW! This is how you start the day," remarked Puff after seeing all the food on the table.

"I agree with you," spoke SarCat after he also saw all the food.

"Good morning to all of you please help yourselves," spoke the King in a cheerful voice.

"Thanks," answered all the Munchkins in unison, they went to the table, sat down, and started to eat breakfast with the King.

After everyone finished eating the King told them, "Now let us go outside and get you on your way to the Warlock's castle."

He then stood up from the table and walked to the doorway, as he approached the door it opened, showing the dawn rays of the beach. The King walked out the large door towards the dock, followed by the Munchkins, SarCat and a few AilSharks. In the lake, a few more AilSharks were swimming, pulling the wagon with rope and soon reached the dock. Once at the dock, more AilSharks came over tying the wagon to it. The King gave the Munchkins some last-minute advice about the lake and the danger of the river that travels near Warlock's castle and the Evil Forest. The Munchkins thanked the King for all his help and climbed back into the wagon. The sun was up, and Mikey turned on the power to the wagon and it started to pull away from the dock. The King waved to them and yelled out, "I ordered some of my AilSharks to escort you as far as they can!"

"Thank you," Mikey yelled back, he waved along with everyone else in the wagon. Mikey looked at the sun and said to Zee, "We only have to sunset to break the Warlock's curse."

Zee looked at him saying, "Somehow we will make it!"

CHAPTER 15

THE HIDDEN ENTRANCE

After some time following the AilSharks escorts, Mikey asked Zee, "How much longer before we reach the other side of this lake?"

Zee took out the map and studied it for a minute then said, "I think we should see land soon and then we look for a small river going into the Evil Forest."

"What about the Warlock's underground castle, are we close?" Mikey asked.

"The map doesn't say, it just tells us to follow the river until we hear the sound of thunder," answered Zee.

Puff shouted, "Land just ahead."

The AilSharks swam over to the wagon and one spoke, "This is as far as we can go, the lake ends near and a small river goes through the Evil Forest, somewhere in there is a hidden entrance to the Warlock's underground castle. Now we must return home, good luck Munchkins." The escorts splashed their tails in the water and disappeared.

"Thanks!" Zee yelled to the AilSharks. She then looked forward towards the land; there were many tall trees on the lake banks, no beach.

"Hey, look at those pretty ducks," Maria pointed out. The ducks were fishing just off the banks of the lake, when they heard the paddle wheel hitting the water they started to swim towards land. Maria watched them as they disappeared into some tall weeds sticking out of the water. Maria said, "Hey, those ducks know where the river starts."

Mikey looked at the tall weeds and said, "I think you're right Maria," He turned the steering wheel and pointed the wagon toward the tall weeds. It was a long time before the wagon reached the weeds. Mikey said, "Everyone stop paddling, we must coast through those tall weeds, or we will get stuck." The wagon slowly made its way into the tall weeds.

"I can't see anything in these weeds," remarked Zee.

"Well, we are still floating and haven't hit land yet, that is a good thing," SarCat spoke. It was not long before the wagon entered the small river.

"Great job Maria! You were right, the ducks know where the river flows," Mikey happily said to her.

"That is my girl," remarked SarCat as he jumped into Maria's lap. The small river water started to flow faster.

Zee pointed ahead saying, "Look, there is the bend in the river." Shortly after the wagon entered the bend in the river; it was not long after that when everyone heard thunder.

SarCat looked up towards the sky and remarked, "I don't see any rain clouds."

"The noise is coming from that fog bank just ahead," Mikey said. Puff's eyes started to tear up, and then he let out one big sneeze.

"I knew it, danger is coming!" SarCat shouted.

Maven looked down at the river current and said, "The water is really moving now."

The wagon entered the fog, as it did the thunder became louder. "I know what is making that noise," SarCat stated panicky.

"What is making that noise?" Maria asked.

"A waterfall," SarCat answered.

Mikey now seeing through the fog sees the waterfall, he tried to drive the wagon to the banks of the river, but the current was just too strong. "I can't steer the wagon; we need to get out of here fast!" Mikey shouted at everyone. Maven quickly stood up on his seat and looked to the riverbank; there he saw a large falling tree lying in the water.

"I have an idea," Maven pronounced.

"Good, hurry up before we go over the falls and become fish food," SarCat warned.

Maven took out his bow and tied one of his arrows to a long rope and the other end to the wagon, and then he pointed the bow at another tree just in front of the one laying in the water. He fired his arrow at the tree; it flew high in the air, carrying the rope and hitting sticking into the tree.

"GREAT SHOT MAVEN!" Granny shouted. Everyone cheered Maven.

"Thanks," Maven replied and yelled, "Hold on!" Everyone grabbed onto the wagon, soon it passed the tree with the arrow stuck into it, as it did the rope

66

tightened, stopping the wagon hard and pulling it to the bank of the river towards the fallen tree lying in the water.

Mikey now knew what Maven was up to and ordered, "Once the wagon hits that tree in the water, everyone jump out with your backpacks and quickly climb onto it and make your way to land." The wagon swung over, hitting the tree, the girls climbed out of the wagon first, followed by the boys and SarCat. A minute later the rope popped, and the wagon drifted away towards the waterfall. The Munchkins and SarCat could only watch as their friend, the wagon, floated over the edge of the waterfall out of site. A loud bang was heard from the wagon hitting the rocks below.

Zee looked at Mikey, "I am sorry that wagon was your greatest invention."

"Thanks," Mikey responded, "Let's get off this tree before we go over the falls and don't forget to take your backpacks."

Once everyone climbed off the fallen tree and reached the safety of land, SarCat whispered, "I will take a look around, wait here." He ran into the thick woods and disappeared.

"Be careful," Maria said.

"I will mother!" SarCat said from the woods.

Mikey smiled, "Let's take a break here until SarCat gets back."

"That was a close call!" Zee remarked as she sat down looking at the fog coming from the waterfalls nearby. It was not long before everyone was resting and thinking about how close they came to death. Granny was having a tough time catching her breath; Zee looked at her and asked in a worried voice, "Are you alright, Granny?"

"Yes, granddaughter, I am just a little tired, don't worry about me, we must save our people and the Good Witch of the North no matter what." Everyone looked at Granny and knew something was wrong but said nothing.

SarCat came back, "I found a pathway, let's get going before anything else happens!" Everyone stood up.

"Good job SarCat, lead the way," Maria said.

SarCat smiled, "Follow me," he turned around and walked back into the thick woods followed by the rest of the Munchkins in a single line. After a few minutes SarCat made his way out of the thick woods along with the Munchkins. "Over there is the pathway I was telling you about, pointing straight ahead."

Everyone walked over to the pathway; Mikey knelt and studied the tracks in the dirt. "It looks like a lot of things travel this pathway," he said nervously.

"Like what?" Puff inquired.

"I don't know but it looks like a lot of them," Mikey responded, "But look on the bright side, the only thing that made those tracks are evil creatures and are most likely going to the Warlock's castle."

Mikey started walking the pathway following the tracks, the other Munchkins followed. It was only a short distance when the group came to the end of the pathway and some incredibly old-looking trees. SarCat walked in front of Mikey and looked at the trees ahead.

"I do not like the looks of those trees! They are scary looking," SarCat stated.

Puff stood next to him, "I think ugly and evil too!"

Suddenly a mist formed around the trees, a voice from one of the trees demanded, "Who are you and why do you call us ugly?"

Another tree said, "Who are you calling scary looking and evil?"

Granny said, "Please forgive us, we mean no harm, only to find the hidden way to the Warlock's castle."

"Only evil goes to the Warlock's castle, are you of evil beings?" The trees questioned.

"No," remarked SarCat, "We came to fight the Warlock for what he did to the Good Witch of the North and the Munchkin people."

"We have heard about that news," spoke the oldest tree in a slow deep voice. "We tree's once long-ago lived-in sunshine and in peace before the Warlock built his underground castle near our land and turned all this land into evil and death. Only creatures live in this land now and travel this pathway on their way to the Warlock's castle," the tree continued, "I can tell that you Granny are old and wise like us and all of you have hearts of good not evil."

Granny looked at the talking tree and smiled, "I think that I am the oldest one here so that makes me the wisest one here." The tree laughed after hearing her talk. As they were laughing, the mist faded away showing a large hole in the ground in the center of the trees.

Mikey asked the trees, "Is that the hidden entrance to the Warlock's castle?"

"Yes, but you don't want to go down there," another tree said still laughing. "Only evil goes into that entrance."

Granny looked at Mikey and the rest of the Munchkins and asked, "How about it my brave friends, are you ready to go face that Warlock and save our friends and loved one?"

"YES!!!" They all shouted.

Granny begged the older tree, "Please old wise tree, will you help us?"

All the trees stopped laughing while the oldest said, "The Warlock is not our friend, we will help you, go stand next to the hole that is in the center of us."

"Thank you!" Granny replied. So, Granny walked towards the hole.

Mikey excitedly said, "Let's follow Granny." As soon as they reached the large hole and stood in front of it, they noticed that the hole was close to twenty feet wide and had a foul smell rising from it and it was deeper than the eye could see.

SarCat looked down in the hole, "How are we going to get down there?"

"Don't worry about that, I can help you," spoke a nearby tree. The large tree let out a loud roar; it pulled up on of its long thick roots from underground and lifted it high in the air. When the root fell back to the ground it landed in the hole traveling all the way to the bottom making a loud banging sound. The tree spoke again, "Use my root as a ladder and climb down."

"Thank you! This will save us time," Granny responded. She then looked at the teenage Munchkins and said, "Before we go any further, I would like to say that I am very proud of each one of you and so is everyone in Munchkin town, no matter what happens down there."

"Thanks Granny," remarked SarCat, "Now let's get going," he jumped onto the tree root.

Mikey pulled out a fire stick from his backpack; he rubbed it on the tree root as he did the fire stick lit up. Mikey dropped it in the hole, the fire stick fell downwards lighting up the hole as it did and the ground below.

SarCat looked down at the light below and commented, "That is better, now we can see where we are climbing." He then started to climb down the tree root ladder leading the way.

The rest of the Munchkins slowly climbed onto the root and started to follow SarCat downward toward the small light at the bottom of the hole. The root made a great ladder and after everyone reached the ground safely, the tree root pulled upwards out of site. Mikey picked up the fire stick and raised it up showing where they were. They were inside a large cave that had one tunnel, inside the walls were hanging torches lighting the way.

"Look a tunnel, it must lead to the Warlock castle," remarked Maria.

"Well, let's find out, we are running out of time," spoke Granny and began to walk quickly down the tunnel followed by the rest of the brave Munchkins.

The Munchkins advanced slowly trying not to make any noise. "Keep your eyes open for those Dragon soldiers," Granny whispered. As they made their way down the tunnel, they could hear singing.

Granny was the first to reach the end of the tunnel and whispered, "Oh NO!" The rest of the Munchkins stood beside her and watched while hundreds of Dragon soldiers marched and sung their favorite song.

"O, O, OREO, OREO." The tunnel opened into an enormous cave that was big enough for Warlock's castle that stood over ten stories high and had many other buildings for his evil friends and allies.

Mikey now took charge, "Everyone, get down so we are not spotted and let's make our way to those large rocks." The Munchkins hurried and made their way to the rocks without any Dragon soldiers seeing them. They slowly raised their heads-up peeping over the rocks and could now see the Warlock Castle that they have been trying for days to find.

"It looks like the Dragon soldiers are getting ready for something," whispered Maven.

"It looks like they are getting ready for war!" Mikey replied.

"But who are they going to fight?" Maria asked.

"Everyone that stands for good in all the lands above ground," Granny said in a worried tone. Mikey looked and studied Warlock castle trying to figure out a way into it without being seen by the army of Dragon soldiers.

CHAPTER 16

WARLOCK CASTLE

Suddenly, the Dragon soldiers stopped marching and singing, they stood at attention in front of the castle waiting for something. "Hey, look at the doors of the castle," spoke Maven. Everyone watched as the large wooden doors slowly opened. Behind the doors walked out a tall man dressed in black wearing a red cape with a golden chain around his neck attached to it was his medallion.

The Dragon soldiers lowered their heads as the Warlock walked out of the castle towards them, he stopped just in front of them and said, "We are almost ready to go aboveground and rule all of the four lands."

"Is that the Warlock?" Maria asked.

"Oh Yea! That is him," answered SarCat.

"Boy he sure is evil looking!" Remarked Zee.

"Look around his neck, it is the medallion," spoke Puff.

The Warlock spoke in a loud voice that traveled throughout his evil kingdom, "Soon, we will travel aboveground and rule the four lands, North, South, East and West." The sounds of hundreds of Dragon soldiers cheered their master and banged their tails shaking the walls of the cave. The Warlock raised up one of his hands in the air to quiet his army. He sensed something was wrong, looking down beyond his army he noticed a small head peeking up from behind a group of large rocks.

Mikey ducked down and whispered, "I think he saw me."

"How do you know?" SarCat asked in a worried way.

"I see you! Come out, come out!!" Warlock shouted.

"See, I told you he seen me." Mikey remarked. All the Munchkins knelt together.

Puff asked, "Who do you think he is talking too?"

Everyone just looked at him while SarCat answered, "I'll give you one guess."

"Munchkins! Come out from behind those rocks or I will have my Dragon soldiers drag you to me!!" The Warlock ordered.

"Well, look on the bright side," remarked SarCat.

Maria looked at him and asked, "How can there be a bright side, the Warlock has found us!"

"The cat is right!" Granny whispered, "This is a way for us to get into the castle." Granny stood up and said, "Let me speak on behalf of the Munchkins. Mikey and the rest of the teenagers looked at Granny and agreed. Granny walked out first from behind the rocks followed by the rest of the brave group.

"Welcome! To my kingdom." spoke the Warlock as they slowly approached him. The Dragon soldiers moved out of their way as they walked by and smiled. "I wish they would stop smiling at us," remarked Zee. They stopped in their tracks about twenty paces from Warlock.

"Why do you risk life coming here?" Warlock asked.

"You know why we are here!" Shouted Granny and then she took two steps forward leaving the teenagers behind her.

"Yes, I think so," replied Warlock. "You wish to destroy me and break the spell I placed on your town, is that it?"

"Do not forget about the Good Witch of the North, you remember her, she was a girlfriend of yours a long time ago, at least that is the way I heard it. But she dumped you when you turned evil." The Warlock did not like the way Granny was speaking to him and was starting to get angry with each word.

Mikey whispered to Granny, "What are you doing? He is getting mad!"

Granny turned her head backward and whispered, "Trust me." Then she winked at him.

You know a lot for an old woman," the Warlock spoke in a low and bitter tone.

Granny turned her head back to the Warlock, "I am old enough to have seen a house from another land fall from the sky killing your sister the Witch of the East."

The Warlock questioned, "So you were there?"

"Yes!" Granny answered. "I was also around when your other sister the Witch of the West was melted away with a bucket of water by our beloved hero, Dorothy of Kansas." Granny knew she was getting the Warlock upset and continued, "Those two evil Witches deserved everything that they got, as you will in due time!" Granny's body rose up into the air, she then flew straight into the hand of the Warlock, and he grabbed her throat.

"LET HER GO!!" Zee screamed. Zee and the rest of the Munchkins started to run at Warlock, but they were suddenly stopped and held in place by Dragon soldiers. The Warlock smiled as he looked into Granny's eyes and slowly choked her to death. Then he dropped Granny's body to the ground and looked over at the rest of the Munchkins being held by Dragon soldiers.

"Who is next?" The Warlock demanded. The Munchkins were in shock after seeing Granny get murdered and did not know what to do. They fell to their knees in disbelief.

CHAPTER 17

HELP HAS COME

Warlock slowly approached the huddled group of frightened Munchkins; in his eyes you could see the hate and anger that had built up inside of him over the past seventy-five years of waiting to revenge his sister's murders. He only took a few steps before a brilliant blue star shaped radiated near the entrance of the cave. It slowly flew towards the Munchkins and landed next to them. The blue light turned into a tall handsome well-dressed man who was holding a golden pocket watch in one hand. It was obvious that it meant a great deal to him.

The man spoke, "Have no fear my young friends, the Good Wiz is here!"

The Munchkins looked up at him puzzled, while SarCat looked at him and asked, "What is a Good Wiz?'

"I am the brother of the Good Witch of the North," replied Good Wiz. "My sister told me what happened, and I am here to join you in the fight against the Warlock."

The Warlock cordially welcomed the Good Wiz, "Well, it is about time you got here. I was wondering if you were ever going to make an appearance, but you are a fool for coming to my castle."

Good Wiz faced the Warlock and remarked, "We will see very soon who the fool is!"

"Well, it's been a long time since our last meeting," remarked Warlock.

"Yes indeed, over a hundred years!" answered Good Wiz. "Now that we had our small talk, I like to give you one last chance to reverse the spell you cast over my sister and the Munchkins before you are destroyed. The Warlock smiled then started to laugh at the Good Wiz.

After he stopped laughing, he said, "You really think that I would reverse my spell and let you get out of here alive!"

"Absolutely, and without a doubt," the Good Wiz smiled confidently.

The Warlock felt insulted and challenged, "It is impossible for you alone to beat me, also my Dragon soldiers. I will destroy you and all the good that you represent, and then I shall rule all of the four lands above forever!" This time the Good Wiz joined him with laughter, when the Warlock heard him laughing, he stopped and yelled at him, "WHY, ARE YOU LAUGHING!"

"Because you think that I would come here all alone!" The Good Wiz laughed.

"Who is going to help you?" questioned Warlock as he looked around.

"I've invited some of your old friends to join me here," Good Wiz chuckled, and then he opened up his pocket watch and looked at the time saying, "They should be here any minute now."

"What friends?" The Warlock inquired in a puzzled way. "I don't have any friends."

You could hear SarCat in the background, "I wonder why?"

The rest of the Munchkins now stood up and snickered at what SarCat said. Mikey stated, "Everyone get out your weapons and let us get ready to fight and pay him back for what he just did to Granny!

Good Wiz smiled at Mikey, then pointed to the rear of the cave saying, "They are here!" Out from the darkness advanced scores of Snow Tigers and AilSharks marching forward in support of the Munchkins and Good Wiz. SarCat could see in the distance that some AilSharks were riding on the backs of Snow Tigers.

"Hey! Look everyone here come my cousins and the AilSharks! There must have be hundreds of them," stated SarCat.

Warlock was shocked as he saw the two armies coming and remembered the curse, he had decades earlier cast on the AilSharks and the Snow Tigers. The curse that changed and prevented the AilSharks from exiting the water within one mile of their island home and the Snow Tigers living only in chilly weather. He looked at both armies puzzled and thought aloud, "How are they surviving?"

Good Wiz overheard his comment, "Because, I cast a counter spell over your spell, neutralizing your spell, so they would be able to join in the fight against you and the Dragon soldiers here today!" The Dragon soldiers released the

Munchkins and slowly backed away from them until they and the rest of the Dragon soldiers stood behind their master and waited for his orders.

Now both the AilSharks and the Snow Tigers reached Good Wiz and the Munchkins, they lined up behind them forming a battle line. After seeing this, the Warlock ordered his Dragon soldiers to line up forming their battle lines directly opposite from them. Soon, both good and evil were poised and ready for battle, each waiting for the command to attack! One flying Dragon Soldier returned from the mission the Warlock sent him on earlier and landed beside the Warlock. He walked over to the Warlock and whispered something in his ear. The Warlock smiled as he heard the news, he addressed the Good Wiz, "Do not think that you are the only one who can invite guests to this battle between Good and Evil. I have invited some guest of my own!" The Warlock looked up, patches of dirt and stones fell from the top of the cave. Countless numbers of Lizard Snakes started to drop down from the ceiling landing behind the readied Dragon soldier's battle line.

Then a loud buzzing sound came from behind the Warlock castle high in the air. It was the Queen of the Puffy bugs along with her swarm of over a hundred bugs. They flew out of a secret tunnel high in the cave. The Queen and her swarm quickly flew behind the battle lines of the Good; they hung in midair blocking the only way out from the cave. Now, Good Wiz, AilSharks, Snow Tigers and the five Munchkin teenagers with one cat were surrounded. Good Wiz looked at the Warlock, then at his armies of evil and said, "It looks like our armies are evenly matched.

Why don't we find out which one of us is stronger?"

"How do we do that?" The Warlock inquired.

"Let us battle inside your castle to the death, the old way, without the use of our power sources, your medallion against my pocket watch, winner takes all."

The Warlock was surprised by the Good Wiz's offer and thought about it for a moment, then replied, "I agree and will enjoy killing you with my own bare hands. I will wait for you inside the castle, say goodbye to your friends," In a puff of some the Warlock had disappeared.

Good Wiz turned to the faces of the Munchkins, "I am sorry about Granny, it took longer than I hoped on getting here," he walked over to Zee and hugged her saying, "Your Granny was a good friend of mine and both of my sisters, she will not be forgotten! Now, please listen to what I am about to tell you, my sister has a plan to defeat the Warlock, but it is going to take all of us working together to make it work!"

Mikey took a step towards Good Wiz, "Whatever the plan is count us in!"

Snow Tiger Queen also stepped forward. AilSharks King walked over to Good Wiz and the Munchkins. "Glad to see you all made it here on time." remarked Good Wiz.

"Thanks! It is great to see you Munchkins again." The AilSharks King replied. They both smiled and hugged. The AilSharks King stood beside the Munchkins and the Good Wiz.

Snow Tiger Queen looked at SarCat and said, "It is great to see you again cousin!"

The AilSharks King spoke, "I along with my AilSharks welcome the chance to battle those Dragon soldiers again. I also bought special weapons that the Good Wiz asked me to bring while he was on our island the other day. The King sat down a large black bag that he was carrying in front of the Munchkins.

"Very good, my dear King," said the Good Wiz, then he turned to the four Munchkins beside him, "You four Munchkins except Mikey, after I go inside the castle reach into that bag and pull out one special pole that will help you in the battle to come."

Mikey looked at Good Wiz, "Don't I get one?"

"Sorry Mikey, I have only so much power. I could only make four of them, besides your fight is getting inside the castle. "Mikey smiled and agreed.

"Now listen to the plan," whispered the Good Wiz. Everyone huddled closer together so they could hear him. "I will go battle the Warlock inside the castle while the army of the AilSharks battles the Dragon soldiers keeping them busy and when the time comes make sure Snow Tiger Queen has a clear pathway to the castle," stated Good Wiz. The King of the AilSharks nodded his head in agreement.

Good Wiz then turned to the Snow Queen Tiger, "Give me four of your best warriors to protect the Munchkins. The last part of this plan is that you will bring Mikey to me in the castle when I summons you. I am counting on you to make sure he gets to me fast and safe." The Snow Tiger Queen nodded her head in agreement. "Now Mikey, get on the Queen's back and have your friends ride on the back of the four Snow Tigers coming with us. Mikey agreed. Good Wiz took Mikey aside from the rest so he could talk to him alone, "Mikey, you have the most important job of all."

"ME?" Mikey questioned nervously.

"YES! You, my boy. Are you still holding the earring my sister gave to you?"

Mikey reached into his pocket and pulled out the earring, "You mean this?"

"That is it!" remarked the Good Wiz happily. "You ride with the Snow Tiger Queen and use that backpack and that invention that is built into it, when you get inside the castle. It is most important! Give that earring to Warlock when you see him. Now, I must go! Good luck to all of us." The Good Wiz turned into a blue star and flew towards the castle, straight into one of the open windows on the top level of the Warlock's castle.

CHAPTER 18

GOOD VS EVIL
BATTLE OF TIME

Mikey watched the window Good Wiz flew into and looked in his hand at the earring the Good Witch of the North gave to him and wondered why it was so important and why he had to give it back to the Warlock. Snow Tiger Queen walked over to Mikey, "Get on my back, we have a job to do!"

Mikey smiled at her and put the earring back inside his pocket then he grabbed his backpack with his last and only invention left, tied it tightly to his back and climbed onto Snow Tiger Queen's back, "I am ready to go!" Snow Queen walked back to where the rest of the Munchkins were waiting along with the armies of AilSharks and Snow Tigers. Mikey looked at his friends, "Well guys, in a few minutes this battle will begin, I just would like to say, no matter what happens next I am so glad that I have friends like you in my life."

Zee smiled at him and replied, "We all feel the same about you!"

SarCat sitting on Maria's lap shouted, "OK, THAT IS ENOUGH TALK! Mikey what is our battle plan going to be?"

Mikey looked at SarCat, "You are right my friend, Let us get ready for the attack, when the time comes, we will split up, Zee and Puff it will be your job to battle those Puffy bugs behind us, take the Snow Tigers and make sure they do not get by you! Maven and SarCat battle along with the AilSharks against the Dragon soldiers and Lizard Snakes."

"Okay!" Everyone replied in one loud voice. Then each one of the four Munchkins walked over to the bag on the ground and pulled out one long pole that was inside. The poles were about five feet long made from strong light wood that had a hand size diamond on one of its ends. Zee and Puff took their poles and looked at them smiling.

Two Snow Tigers walked beside them and stated, "Climb on!" As soon as they were on, the two Snow Tigers slowly turned around and started to walk towards the back of the battle line with the rest of the army of good. The swarm of Puffy killer bugs still hovering in the air were blocking the way out of the cave.

The Queen spotted them coming and ordered the swarm to get ready to sting. The swarm quickly lowered their long stingers and got ready to attack. At the same time Maven and Maria were next to grab the poles out of the black bag Good Wiz made.

Two more Snow Tigers walked beside them saying, "Climb on!" They climbed up onto their backs with their poles, SarCat then jumped on Maria's lap.

SarCat said, "Don't worry, my cousins won't let any harm come to you!"

The two Snow Tigers walked over and joined the other two Snow Tigers already standing in line. Now, the four Munchkins were armed with a magic pole that they had no idea how to use, they stayed in place in the battle line along with the AilSharks King, his soldiers and the army of the Snow Tigers facing the battle line of the Dragon soldiers and the Snake Lizards. Both armies stood and stared at each other without saying a word, each side waited for the order to attack the other. Mikey and the Queen of the Snow Tigers stood nearby and waited for Good Wiz to call them.

In Warlock's castle, in the biggest room, it was over five stories high and could hold over a hundred Dragon soldiers at any time, had a large fireplace that was always burning red hot. Warlock watched as the blue star came through the open window and land near him. Good Wiz appeared holding his pocket watch in one hand.

"Welcome to my home! Sorry it can be the only visit since you are never leaving this room alive! Warlock snickered. "I won't be as easy to beat as my sister's."

"Let us see how strong you are when it is a man you are fighting!" Good Wiz remarked as he slowly walked towards Warlock.

Warlock was sitting in his favorite chair made of bones of dead enemies. He stood up, "I asked her to leave but she refused to leave her beloved Munchkins, I did not want to fight her. BUT YOU! I will not hold back, after you are dead, nobody will ever challenge me again!"

"Now, let us put aside your medallion and my pocket watch and see who the better man is, shall we?" Suggested the Good Wiz.

"I have been waiting to kill you for many years," spoke the Warlock as he stood up from his chair, he pulled his medallion from around his neck and placed it on a small table beside his chair. He then walked to the center of the room and waited for Good Wiz.

Good Wiz smiled at the Warlock thinking to himself, "I need to stay alive long enough to get Mikey's help in here and for him to grab that medallion." He walked over to the table and place his pocket watch beside the Warlock's medallion. He then walked over to Warlock and stood face to face with him. Warlock was taller and bigger than Good Wiz, but he was not as fast as him.

"Now, before we find out who is the better man and I take your life, let me start the battle outside," remarked the Warlock. He yelled in a voice that could be heard throughout the entire cave, "ATTACK! Kill all the AilSharks, Snow Tigers and Munchkins!

Good Wiz did not have to yell out any orders, his armies of good knew what they had to do and were waiting for the armies of Evil to attack.

"Are you done talking?" The Good Wiz asked.

Warlock looked at him, "Yes, why?"

Good Wiz remarked, "Good, then he threw the first punch hitting the Warlock hard on the chin.

The Warlock smiled at him, rubbed his chin, "You are going to have to hit harder than that to beat me," he remarked, then he jumped on the Good Wiz, and both were now in a hand-to-hand fight to the death.

Just outside the castle, both armies were ready for battle when they heard Warlock order the attack. The Dragon soldiers, Snake Lizards and Puffy bugs started to attack. The Dragon soldier's general yelled, "CHARGE!" The battle line of hundreds ran and jumped into the air toward the battle line of armies of Good while the Snake Lizards moved slowly straight behind the Dragon soldiers waiting for the chance to get back at the Munchkins. The Queen Puffy bug slowly flew towards the line of the army of good, her swarm close behind her, she and her swarm had their stingers out ready to kill anything in their way.

"HERE THEY COME! Shouted Mikey to everyone in the long battle line of the armies of good.

The King of the AilSharks yelled, "LET'S GET THEM BOYS!" Then he started to run towards the oncoming Dragon soldiers followed by every one of his AilSharks soldiers including Maven, Maria and SarCat riding on the backs of two Snow Tigers.

Zee turned around along with all the Snow Tigers and shouted, "LET'S KILL SOME BUGS!"

The two Snow Tigers that were carrying Zee and Puff started to run towards the swarm of Puffy bugs, all the Snow Tigers were close behind running with their claws out. Within a few minutes, hundreds of Dragon soldiers, Snake Lizards, and giant Puffy bugs were in a battle with

AilSharks, Snow Tigers, four Munchkins and a tough cat. Snow Tiger Queen and Mikey stayed in place and waited for Good Wiz to summon them; they watched the battle going on all around them. Inside the castle, the Warlock and Good Wiz were fighting hand to hand without any help of magic from their pocket watch or medallion. Good Wiz was finding out that Warlock was stronger and knew he could not beat him in a long fight.

"I must think of a way to get Mikey in here soon," Good Wiz thought.

The Warlock stood back up, Good Wiz slowly stood up and looked up at the open window high up behind him and thought to himself, "That is it! If Snow Queen can get Mikey to that open window in time!" He then closed his eyes and called Snow Tiger Queen, "Bring Mikey to me now, use the same window as I." That was all he could sent out, Warlock jumped and kicked Good Wiz in his chest. He flew across the large room hitting the brick wall on the other side. "You're no match for me!" stated Warlock as he walked towards the Good Wiz still laying against the wall. The Good Wiz tried to stand up but fell back down holding his ribs. The Warlock laughed, "I think you have a few broken ribs."

The Good Wiz tried to stand up again, this time he made it up and remarked, "Going to take more than a few broken ribs to beat me! He prepared for another attack from Warlock.

The Snow Tiger Queen heard the message from Good Wiz, she turned her head to see Mikey on her back and said, "It is time, Good Wiz needs us now!"

Both armies were now battling all around. The Snow Tigers along with Zee and Puff were fighting the Puffy bugs. Zee was the first Munchkin to use one of the magic poles Good Wiz made. She aimed at one Puffy bug coming at her, the diamond lit up shooting a white beam of light from it. The Puffy bug just disappeared out of site and the fight.

"WOW! Did you see that?" Puff stated after seeing Zee use the pole. "So, that is how it works, just point at the bad guys and they disappear."

The Snow Tigers were jumping up at the Puffy bugs with their claws wide open, their claws ripping them apart as they grabbed them. The Puffy bugs outnumbered the Snow Tigers five to one, they used their numbers to attack the Snow Tigers on all sides. After they stung a Snow Tiger, they soon fell to the ground slowly dying. Puff and Zee used the magic pole hitting as many as he could while trying to avoid the stingers of hundreds of Puffy bugs.

Both sides fighting hard, Zee yelled to Puff beside him, "WE NEED TO HOLD THEM!"

"I KNOW!" Puff replied while still shooting his magic pole.

Just a short distance behind the battle with the Snow Tigers, the Dragon soldiers and AilSharks were in another tough fight, both soldiers were evenly matched. There were dozens of fights going on in front of the Snow Tiger Queen and Mikey. Dragon soldiers were now spitting fireballs at the AilSharks, when they hit one, they caught fire and were put out of the battle. Maven and Maria also found out how to use their magic poles and were knocking many of the Dragon soldiers out of battle.

The Snow Tiger Queen told Mikey to hold on to her neck collar. Mikey put both hands on the collar and yelled, "LET'S GO FOR IT!" The Queen jumped ahead and started running into the battle lines of the Dragon soldiers and AilSharks. Mikey held on tight while the Queen ran by the soldiers fighting. The AilSharks King and two of his soldiers ran beside her and Mikey helping to clear the way to the castle ahead. A flying group of six Dragon soldiers attacked the AilSharks King and his two soldiers.

The Snow Tiger Queen dove out of the way and got away and made it to the side of the castle out of sight of any Dragon soldiers or Snake Lizards.

"Great job Queen! You made it to the castle without getting caught," Mikey said.

"Thanks, we were lucky, now Good Wiz told me to come in the same window he did." They both looked up at the castle walls.

Mikey pointed to the window, "THAT IS IT!"

CHAPTER 19

LOVE CAN KILL

That window was five stories high. "How are we going to get up there?" Mikey inquired.

"You let me worry about that, just hold on to my collar again." The Queen Tiger replied. She then opened every claw on her four large paws. Mikey held on while she stood up on her back two legs then with her claws out, she started climbing the castle wall towards the open window where the Good Wiz flew. It only took a few minutes to climb the castle wall, and they were halfway there.

Mikey could now see the entire battlefield, it looked like the evil army was now winning and soon would defeat the army of good, he remarked in a worried voice, "Did you plan on those two flying Dragon soldiers coming at us?"

The Snow Tiger Queen turned her head to see where they were, then she looked up at the open window and thought to herself, "I'll never make it there in time." The Snow Tiger Queen started climbing faster, as she climbed, she told Mikey, "My dear, we only have a minute before they attack, no matter what happens to me, remember your loved ones, the Good Witch and Granny are counting on you!"

Mikey was about to answer her, but he soon heard her let out a loud painful scream. He turned back to see her and saw two Dragon soldiers pulling each one of her back legs, their large hands also had claws and they were stuck in her, blood coming out fast, covering her white fur slowly red.

"Where do you think you are going?" A Dragon soldier laughed as he pulled harder on her beg.

"LET ME GO!" Ordered the Snow Tiger Queen.

"I don't think so," answered another Dragon soldier, "We got you! You and that Munchkin kid will soon be dead from the long fall you are about to take." Both

Dragon soldiers laughed together and flapped their wings backwards pulling harder on the Snow Tiger Queen's legs.

"Mikey, I can't hold on much longer, you must jump up to the window and climb in," she painfully told him.

"Let me help you!" Mikey begged.

"No!" The Queen ordered, "Get to that window or everything will be lost forever!"

Mikey knew she was speaking the truth and looked back up to the window, it was close but still too far away for him to jump with his backpack on. "I can't make it," Mikey told her.

"I'll get you a little closer," The Queen replied, "You climb onto my shoulders and jump up when I say so and grab the window edge and pull yourself up." She then used only her front two paws and slowly climbed upwards on the castle wall towards the open window, as Mikey made his way to her shoulders.

"Pull harder!" One of the Dragons soldiers said to the other.

They were just too much for the Snow Tiger Queen, she climbed up a few more feet then yelled to Mikey, "I CAN'T HOLD ON ANY LONGER MY FRIEND, GOOD LUCK, NOW JUMP!"

Mikey looked at her and nodded, he then knelt and jumped off upwards towards the open window just above him now. The Snow Tiger Queen watched Mikey as he jumped and grabbed the windows edge with his fingers. Then she turned her head and looked at both Dragon soldiers pulling on her back legs, "You guys pulled on the wrong pair of legs!" She let go of the wall and used her front two paws to attack both Dragon soldiers.

Mikey watched her battle with both Dragon soldiers until they all hit the ground below to their deaths. Mikey yelled, "NO!" His eyes teared up seeing Snow Tiger Queen's dead body lying on the ground below. He turned his head back to the open window and slowly pulled himself up and sat on the window's edge. He could now see Warlock and Good Wiz fighting and a sitting chair with a small table beside it, on the table he saw the pocket watch and the medallion. Mikey smiled as he saw them, thinking to himself, "It is time to use my last invention." The Warlock now had Good Wiz in a choke hold and was slowly killing him. Mikey was nearly seventy-five feet high, and another fifty feet or so away from where the table with the medallion was. He looked at the Warlock and the Good Wiz still fighting, the Warlock now had his entire weight on the back of Good Wiz's neck, he was beginning to turn red, then purple and was about to pass out.

The Warlock knew Good Wiz only had minutes of life left and said, "Your time and life are almost gone, any last words?"

Good Wiz looked up at the open window, saw Mikey, and smiled, he then replied, "That is funny, I was just about to ask you the same thing!" The Warlock was surprised by his answer until he looked up and spotted Mikey in the window getting ready to jump.

"What is that Munchkin doing up there?" The Warlock wondered. This distraction was just the break the Good Wiz was waiting for, he slipped his body down breaking free of the Warlock's choke hold. He then maneuvered his body under the Warlock's legs and emerged from behind him putting a headlock on him. The Warlock could not move his arms or legs in any direction. Good Wiz for the first time had the edge, he said to the Warlock, "Did you forget old buddy, I was wrestling champ in our high school!"

Good Wiz then looked back up at Mikey and yelled, "USE YOUR INVENTION, NOW! I DON'T KNOW HOW LONG I CAN HOLD HIM!" The Warlock tried to break free of Good Wiz's hold, but he could not, then he saw Mikey look over at his medallion and knew what he was up to.

The Warlock yelled, "DRAGON SOLDIERS GET IN HERE NOW!"

Mikey looked down to where the medallion was and said to himself, "Boy, I sure hope this invention works as good as all my other ones did or this will be my last!" He then jumped off the windows edge and pulled a string that was coming out from his backpack. Two short wings popped out from the sides of the backpack. Mikey now had wings and was flying down and gliding across the room towards the Warlock's medallion. The Warlock saw Mikey flying towards his medallion and knew he better break free of Good Wiz's hold on him. He made one last try to break free using every bit of his strength, this time he was successful in throwing Good Wiz backward to the ground.

Warlock started to run as fast as he could across the room towards his medallion trying to beat Mikey there. Mikey had the lead, but the Warlock was closing in on him fast. Mikey landed near the Warlock's chair, he quickly looked behind him and saw the Warlock coming at him, so he reached into his pocket and pulled out the earring that the Good Witch of the North gave him three days ago, with his other hand he grabbed the Warlock's magic medallion and put it around his neck shouting, "I GOT IT!"

The Warlock opened his mouth wide and yelled, "NOOOO!" His thunderous screams could be heard throughout the entire castle and outside, stopping the battle between the armies of good and evil.

Mikey saw the Warlock coming at him with his mouth wide open, he quickly remembered what the Good Witch told him, "You must defeat evil from within." Mikey smiled at the Warlock as he now knew what she was talking about; he threw the earring straight at the Warlock's gaping mouth just a few feet away from him, the earring went in his mouth which caused the Warlock to stop in his tracks and swallow the earring. Mikey looked into the Warlock's terrified eyes and said, "That earring is from your old girlfriend, the Good Witch of the North! She wanted you to have it back!" Warlock's body suddenly became limp, and he went down on his knees.

Good Wiz walked over and stood by Mikey putting his hands on his shoulders, "Nice job my boy!"

The Warlock looked at both Mikey and the Good Wiz, "What did you do to me?"

Good Wiz looked at him, "There is one thing that will always defeat evil."

"What's that earring have to do with love?" Asked Warlock.

"Remember, you gave my sister those earrings out of love and now that love will destroy your evil heart and the rest of you!" Good Wiz replied.

The Warlock screamed in pain, "you killed me!" He started to change colors while shrinking down in size. Mikey and Good Wiz watched as he became smaller and smaller, then when he was just the size of an apple there was a flash of red smoke. When the smoke cleared Warlock was gone, he vanished, only the earring remained. Good Wiz knelt and picked up the earring, he looked at it and then gave it back to Mikey. "You hold on to this for now." Good Wiz told him.

Mikey took it and put it back into his pocket, "How could an earring kill the Warlock, he was so powerful?"

"Well Mikey, I will tell you. The Warlock loved my sister very much and during those times his heart was full of good, and that earring was still filled with his love." After he turned evil his heart turned to hate, so when that earring went into his body all that love spilled out and made its way to his heart and the rest of him. His body and heart could not live or stand all that love. Now, let us get out of here, Warlock's spell still must be broken with that medallion by my sister." explained Good Wiz. He reached down and picked up his golden pocket watch and held it in one hand, "Take Mikey and I outside the castle in front of all to see," his pocket watch started to glow then in a puff of smoke both Good Wiz and Mikey were standing in front of hundreds of Dragon soldiers, AilSharks, Snow Tigers, Puffy bugs, Snake Lizards, four Munchkins and one tough cat.

Warlock's army of evil surrendered after seeing Good Wiz and Mikey. The Queen of the Puffy bugs turned backwards and flew away with what was left of her swarm following her. The four teenagers and SarCat ran over to Mikey giving him a big hug and cheering. Good Wiz asked Mikey, "May I hold that medallion for a minute or two."

"Sure," Mikey answered, he pulled off the medallion from around his neck and gave it to Good Wiz.

Good Wiz took Warlock's medallion and raised it over his head, so everyone could see and said, "The evil Warlock is dead! Let all who can see this be free of his evil curse!"

Suddenly the medallion started to spin and flew into the air above all the AilSharks, Snow Tigers, Flying Dragon soldiers and Snake Lizards. The medallion then started to shoot hundreds and hundreds of tiny beams of light at all that were cursed by Warlock. Everyone that was cursed now changed back to their human forms of so long ago.

They looked at themselves and cheered "We are free at last!!"

The medallion returned to Good Wiz's hand, he took it and gave it back to Mikey, "You and the rest of your friends must get back to Munchkin town now, the sun will be setting very soon."

"We will never make it in time," Mikey answered.

"Yes, you and the rest of your friends make a circle and hold hands, say magic words then the medallion will take all of you there in minutes" Good Wiz explained.

"What are the magic words?" Mikey questioned.

"The same ones Dorothy used seventy-five years ago to get back to her home in Kansas. Before you say them, quickly say hello to some of your old friends."

"Wait a minute, you're not coming with us," Mikey asked.

"No, I must take all these people back to their homes but tell my sister I will be over to her castle later." Answered Good Wiz. Soon former AilSharks, Snow Tigers along with changed Dragon soldiers and Snake Lizards came over to thank the Munchkins and Good Wiz for everything they did for them. After a quick visit everyone wished each other goodwill and peace. "Now everyone stand clear of the Munchkins and SarCat," Good Wiz ordered, he gave each one including SarCat a hug, thanking them for all they did, he took a few steps backwards and told Mikey, "Now, make the circle, hold hands and say those magic words."

The Munchkins quickly made a circle and grabbed each other's hands, and then Mikey repeated, "There is no place like home!" Soon after those words the medallion around his neck started to shake then from the center of it a tiny tornado came out and surrounded all the Munchkins and SarCat that was sitting inside the circle. The tornado lifted the Munchkins along with SarCat into the air toward the tunnel exit at the top of the cave. The Munchkins could see below their friends and Good Wiz waving at them as they flew up and out of the cave towards Munchkin town.

Puff was the first to speak, "Boy, how can we be spinning and moving so fast and yet I do not feel dizzy. I feel like I am standing still."

"I don't know how but it is surely a fun ride." Maria stated.

"Hey, look back at the cave we just came from, a rainbow is coming out of it," Maven remarked. Everyone watched the rainbow shoot from the cave upwards into the late afternoon sky.

SarCat noticed that something was inside the rainbow, "What is that inside of the rainbow."

"It is Good Wiz and all the humans he turned back to what they were before. Good Wiz must be taking them all back to their homelands," Mikey explained.

"Hey, look a bright yellow star came out of the rainbow and is coming this way towards us," said SarCat. The yellow star shot by the rainbow; it had a face on it.

"GRANNY!" Zee shouted, "Everyone look!

"She is smiling at us!" Mikey happily said. Everyone smiled at the yellow flying star. Granny winks at them and then flew upward out of site. Mikey affectionately turned to Zee, "Are you alright?"

Zee had glassy eyes but replied, "I am now," and then she gave a big smile while still holding on to his hand.

SarCat saw the way Mikey and Zee were looking at each other and started to cheer, "Mikey's got a girlfriend!

Soon all the Munchkins were also cheering, "Mikey's got a girlfriend!" Zee and Mikey just smiled at each other and said nothing. As the tornado traveled high in the sky it moved at a great speed, faster than any other tornado had done before.

"WOW! "At this speed we will be in Munchkin town in no time," Puff remarked while looking down at the land below. A brief time later, they were looking down at the desert.

"We are getting closer now," Mikey said.

"There is Munchkin town below," SarCat said a few minutes later. The tornado slowed and lowered itself down to the ground landing outside the broken walls that once surrounded the entire town. The high winds subsided then disappeared. The five Munchkins and SarCat were now outside of town.

Mikey looked up at the sun, it was starting to set. "Hurry, we must get to the Good Witch before the darkness touches her!" All of them started to run as fast as they could to the center of town where Glinda and all the folks of Munchkin town were. It did not take long before the group reached the center of town and Glinda. As they walked up to her, they saw that her eyes were closed.

"Wake up Glinda; we are back with the Warlock's medallion." Mikey quickly said to her. Glinda slowly opened her eyes and smiled.

"I knew you guys would make it," Glinda said, "Now hurry, place the Warlock's medallion around my neck before the darkness reaches me." Mikey looked at the darkness coming toward her feet and quickly took the medallion off his neck and reached up and put it around Glinda's neck.

Glinda spoke these words as the medallion wrapped around her neck, "With this medallion I break this spell placed upon me and the one also on all of the Munchkins and their pets!"

The medallion started to shake and glow a bright white light that blinded Mikey and the rest of the teenagers for a moment. After the bright light faded, Mikey and the rest of the Munchkins slowly opened their eyes and smiled at what was in front of them. Glinda was instantly changed back into the beautiful Good Witch of the North she was once before.

"Oh my, my, that is much better," Glinda pronounced as she stretched out her arms. Mikey and the rest of the group ran over to her and gave her a hug and she happily returned a hug to each one thanking them for a job well done. "Now, let's turn my beloved King and the rest of the Munchkins back as they were before the Warlock came to town," Glinda mentioned as she removed the Warlock's medallion from around her neck and laid it on the ground, she pulled out her magic wand from inside her cape and waved it over the medallion, it began to glow brighter and brighter, finally breaking and shattering into a dozen pieces.

Instantly, King Jerry and all the Munchkins along with the animals previously turned into stone statues days ago changed back into their original life forms.

King Jerry and the rest of the Munchkins stood and looked at the Good Witch and the group of teenagers around her and walked over to them, "What happened?" How did the Warlock's spell get broken and where is he now?"

"It is a very long story my dear King, but there will be no more fear of Warlock, he is dead! All in part to this brave group of teenagers, and the leadership of Mikey and his inventions." Glinda stated proudly.

The King smiled at the group and shouted, "DING DONG, THAT WARLOCK IS GONE!" The town folks cheered and ran over to Mikey and the others to thank them including all their parents.

Glinda spoke, "Now, let's see about getting this town back together." She waved her magic wand high in a circular motion at the town, magically the town began to reconstruct and fix itself. All the destroyed buildings and the town walls were mended, in a matter of seconds everything was back to normal. The town looked exactly like it did before Warlock and his Dragon soldiers destroyed it. All the Munchkins cheered after seeing their town back to its beautiful peaceful self.

King Jerry looked at Mikey, "You and the rest of your brave group follow me to the town platform; I want it to be heard about how Warlock was defeated." The King then climbed up the steps to the platform and walked over to his chair.

Mikey, Zee, Maria, Puff and Maven followed him onto the platform. Glinda joined them and a few of the other Munchkins brought chairs for all of them to sit upon.

Once everyone was seated, King Jerry made a speech to the town's people now standing in front of the platform, "On behalf of Munchkin town, I want to thank the Good Witch of the North, our brave teenagers and SarCat for what they have done for us. Just like our heroes of years past, their names will be honored like Dorothy! Their acts of bravery will go down in Munchkin history." King Jerry continued, "It has been told to me that our town lost one of its favorite Munchkins, 'Granny,' gave her life so we all could be here today, she made the ultimate sacrifice. Now, let us give three cheers in Granny's name! "Hip, Hip, Hooray! Hip, Hip, Hooray! Hip, Hip, Hooray!" The entire town's people shouted at the same time.

The King continued when it quieted down a bit, "Now, let us bow our heads in a moment of silence." The King continued after a moment, "I officially dedicate and rename this town square in her name, from this moment on this town square will be known as Granny Square." Everyone let out a cheer, there was not a single dry eye to be found.

Glinda stood up and walked over to King Jerry and whispered something into his ear, he smiled as he listened to what she was telling him. King Jerry looked at Glinda, smiled and nodded his head with approval. King Jerry stood up and faced the town folks and began to address everyone, "Let me have all of your attention please." The town folks became quite so they could hear his words. "The Good Witch and I felt it was about time for me to step down as your king, I have been your king for over seventy-five years now and our town needs young blood to take it into our new future! The town folks could not believe what the King was saying. Glinda walked over to King Jerry and stood beside him in support. King Jerry continued, "With that in mind, I would like to nominate Mikey! Do I have a second?"

Glinda smiled, "I second the motion!

Mikey was awestruck with what he just heard, so were Zee, Puff, Maria, Maven and SarCat. Mikey did not know what to do or say, King Jerry walked over to him, "How about it my boy, would you do us the honor of leading us into the future?"

The entire town started to chant, "Mikey, Mikey!" Soon all his friends were beside him and joining in on the chanting. Mikey looked at the town folks as they continued chanting and cheering for him.

"Everyone is waiting on your answer Mikey, do you want the job?" The King inquired.

Before Mikey could answer, Glinda walked over to him and just like she did to the King, she whispered something into Mikey's ear. He listened to her words and got a surprised look on his face after she had finished.

"Really? You think I should ask her?" Mikey replied to her.

Glinda smiled at him, "Yes, I do!"

Mikey reached into his pocket and pulled out the earring, but he kept his fist closed so it could not be seen by anyone. He then put out his hand in front of the Good Witch and held it up to her. Glinda waved her magic wand over it, his hand started to glow, then it stopped. Mikey looked at his hand, "Is it done?"

"Yes, you can go ask now." Glinda responded.

The town stopped chanting and became quiet and watched Mikey as he walked over to Zee sitting in a chair, he knelt down on one knee and said, "The King needs a Queen, would you like the lifetime job?" He then held out his hand and opened it in front of her. The earring was transformed into the most beautiful diamond ring.

Zee's eyes popped open, and she was awestruck, but she quickly looked up at Mikey and answered "YES!" I would love to be your Queen, my new King." Mikey kissed her.

SarCat shouted, "It looks like Munchkin town has a new King and Queen, long live both of them!"

The whole town cheered and chanted, "Long live the King and Queen."

Mikey took Zee's hand, both walked back and stood beside King Jerry and The Good Witch, "Yes, I will take the job along with my soon to be Queen."

"Great!" King Jerry said with joy, "Now let us get you guys married and you King!"

"Hold on King," Mikey said, "I have one request, we all missed the story you were about to tell before Warlock came to town, it has been a long three days. Can my friends and I just sit here and listen to your story while you are still King and before I become one?"

"Yes, anything for you my future King." King Jerry replied.

Don't miss out!

Visit the website below and you can sign up to receive emails whenever Michael T Ernst publishes a new book. There's no charge and no obligation.

https://books2read.com/r/B-A-WUWGB-OGDBD

BOOKS 2 READ

Connecting independent readers to independent writers.

www.ingramcontent.com/pod-product-compliance
Lightning Source LLC
Chambersburg PA
CBHW060234180626
46813CB00007B/3084